TEMPTING TEACHER

DOMINATING DESIRES
BOOK TWO

MAHI MISTRY

Tempting Teacher

Copyright © 2022 Mahi Mistry

All rights reserved. No part of this book may be reproduced or transmitted in any form or by any electronic or mechanical means, including information storage and retrieval systems, without written permission from the author, except for the use of brief quotations in a book review.
This book is a piece of fiction. Names, characters, places, and incidents are the product of the author's imagination. Any resemblance to actual events, locales, or persons, living or dead, is coincidental.
This book is licensed for your personal enjoyment only.
This book may not be re-sold or given away to other people. If you are reading this book and did not purchase it, or it was not purchased for your use only, then you should return it to the seller and purchase your own copy.
Thank you for respecting the hard work of this author.

Published by Mahi Mistry
Cover Design by GetCovers
Edited by Jeanie Creech
Proofread by Edresa Ramos
ISBN e-Book: 978-93-5526-621-7
ISBN paperback: 978-93-5566-748-9

*Dedicated to readers who loves reading smutty, steamy romances.
Stay Kinky!*

PART I

"I'll reward you with anything you want."

1
MY BUTT IS CUTE

MIA

My best friends were liars. There's nothing fun about being in a cramped, sweaty house bursting full of teenage hormones, loud music, sweat, alcohol, and the burning sharp smell of weed that hangs in the air.

I elbowed my way through the sweaty mob of drunk people and looked for my friends who were eager to try Aaron Matthews' 'new stuff' in his room. It was his house and being the rich kid of the governors of our state meant he could do whatever he wanted when his parents were out of town.

As our school was starting tomorrow, everyone from our year, including the seniors, received a video invitation—yes, a video—to come to his party and get 'smashed.'

I know, kids these days.

"Hey Mia!" I turned around and came face to face with Aaron, the host. His pupils were wide and the whites of his eyes were red.

"Where's Emma and Summer?" I yelled at him because the music was too loud.

"What? Who?"

"Emma and Summer? One of them is dressed as Sailor Moon because she thought this was a costume party." Summer was the only person who would come to a party dressed in a blue skirt and white top with red thigh-highs. Emma had sighed and muttered she doesn't know her when she came to pick us up with her driver. "Are they upstairs?"

Recognition lit his eyes as he nodded. "That blue miniskirt chick? Yeah, she bought a lot of candies. But I don't know where they are." He leaned closer. The smell of weed wafted in my nose as he said in my ear, "My room is empty. Do you want to come over?"

I shook my head. "No, thanks. I don't do drugs."

Turning around, I walked away from him before he could finish his next sentence. I froze in my track when I saw a girl, probably a senior, squealing and running from the kitchen hallway towards the backyard in nothing but denim shorts with her hands covering her... girlie bits.

"I think I've seen enough for a day," I muttered to myself and called Emma for the tenth time in an hour. I shouldn't have agreed to Summer's idea of going to this party, but her puppy eyes were enough to convince me.

The shrill sound of sirens rang through my ears, and my eyes widened. The DJ stopped the music and everyone started scrambling.

"What's happening?" I asked the tipsy girl beside me and helped her up when she tripped.

"Cops are here," she grinned dizzily at me. "The party is moving to Caleb's house, you should come with us!" Cheers went off as the crowd rushed towards the backdoor.

A neighbour must have filed a noise complaint, but if the cops saw us all with drugs and candies—as Aaron liked to call it—we would all be in big trouble. And it was not in my bucket list to get arrested by cops and see the disappointed look on my father's face when he bails me out and then disowns me.

I dialed Summer's number.

"Hello?" Her honeyed voice spoke through the phone.

"Summer! Where are you guys? The cops are here—"

"Ha!" she snickered. "You fell for it, dummy. Send me a voicemail after the *beeeeep*."

I sighed, listening to her mimic a robotic beep and mentally noted to scold her for changing her voicemail. Again. "Call me when you get this. I hope you and Em are safe with Caleb."

Caleb was Emma's boyfriend, and I hadn't seen him run through the panicked and excited crowd of drunk teenagers from the backyard. I was too short and petite to push through the incoming teens and go upstairs. My body was already being pushed through the throngs of people as they all laughed and shrieked in drunken glory. Panic seized me when I heard the cops barging into the house from the front doors, and adrenaline coursed through me with the fear of being disowned by my father.

I stomped and elbowed out of the crowd, running in the opposite direction of the people, sprinting down the other street and thanking past me for wearing run-down Vans and not heels. My heart burned as I took a few deep breaths, trying to calm myself down. I was alone on the empty street.

Then I remembered that my friends could have gone to Caleb's house for the afterparty.

Stupid, stupid Mia.

To make matters worse, rain started pouring, instantly soaking me and my clothes. I cursed, trying to pull the thin blouse from my skin, but it was stuck to me like a glue. I almost called Dad and remembered that he was going to watch a hockey game with his friends and how much he was looking forward to it. I didn't want to disturb him.

That left only one other option. But it's a weekend and he could be on a date, and what if I'm disturbing him, too? Shaking my head, I stood under the shade of a tree. Cold water sluiced down my hair, falling on my crossed arms and making me shiver. I averted my eyes when a pair of two men walked past the other street, eyeing me.

I remembered his words from before. When I had walked downstairs after getting ready for the party. He had looked at me with a frown and said, "Call me if anything happens."

Anything includes getting stranded in the rain, right?

I dialed his number, rubbing my arm to stop the goosebumps. My fancy blouse and shorts were drenched. I didn't want to imagine how my face looked with mascara running down my cheeks.

He picked up on the third ring. His rich, velvety voice purred through my ear, "Where are you?"

Biting my lip from smiling, I rocked on the soles of my shoes and asked, "How did you know I'm in trouble?"

"Are you in trouble?"

"No."

"Then should I go back to my date with Julia, who's waiting for a very special dessert?"

Irritation pricked through my skull, and I regretted calling him. I should've gone to Caleb's house like everyone else. "Oh, shoot. I'm sorry for disturbing your date."

"I'm kidding." Relief poured through me, and I hated that it relieved me when it shouldn't. He was my father's best-friend. It *wasn't* right. "Tell me where you are."

I told him the street name and heard the keys jingling and the door slamming shut through the phone.

"Stay there, princess. I'll be there in ten."

The sound of his smooth voice soothed the panic, and I stayed still even when the rain got harsher. Tiny prickles of shiver climbed up my spine as the rain dribbled faster. I jumped when thunder struck the dark sky, goosebumps skittering all over my body.

I rocked back and forth on my shoes, my heart beating faster as I waited for his car to show up. It was way past my curfew, and just before I could call him again, my phone died.

"This is great," I muttered underneath my breath and bumped into something. My head shot up, and I blinked at the guy standing in front of me. "Sorry."

"Who are you?" I tried to walk beside him, but he held my elbow. His voice was slurred, and he seemed drunk. "What are you doing out here at this hour... wearing *that*?"

"*Excuse me?*" Frowning, I struggled with his hold on my arm, but his fingers tightened on my skin to the point of hurting. "Who the hell are you, trying to hit on an underage girl at this hour?" I clenched my jaw and pulled away, but he didn't budge. "Let me go or I'll scream and kick you in your family jewels so hard that you'll never be able to procreate."

"So you're underage, drunk, and all alone in this rain, drenched in your skimpy top?"

"Thanks, Mister Obvious, but I'm not drunk."

"You're coming with me." The leering smile on his face made me want to puke.

"No, I'm not." I knew kicking him in his balls wouldn't work as he was already dragging me away from the street where I told James I'd be waiting, but I could stomp on his feet as hard as I could.

"Let her go."

I sighed in relief at seeing him standing in front of me. Rain had stopped pouring for a while and the only sound I could hear was the loud hammering of my heart against my ears and my breathing.

"I found her first," the stranger said with a disgusting smirk on his face. "You can get in line."

My jaw dropped hearing his crude words as heat creeped up my neck. I did the only thing I could do. I pinched him. *Hard.* The guy squealed in a high-pitched voice and let go off my arm.

"Disgusting prick." I rubbed the red marks of his fingers on my skin.

A warm coat hugged my shoulders, and I glanced at his sharp face leaning close. "Are you okay, Mia?" His deep blue eyes were concerned and a little angry.

I nodded, too afraid to speak anything at such proximity to his face. His fingers brushed over the red hue on my arm and glared at the guy who was too busy to notice James' sharp look.

I stifled my gasp when he prowled towards him and punched him so hard that he fell down. James held the guy by the collar of his neck and there was blood on the corner of his lips. He said something to him. The stranger's eyes flickered to me in fear as he nodded and James let him go. He scampered away without looking back at us.

"What did you do?" I asked when he grabbed my wrist and took me to his car. I knew he was rich, but I didn't know he was I-can-buy-as-many-electric-and-sports-cars-as-I-want rich. So count me mystified when I saw him unlocking the car door with a card. "What did you tell him?"

His eyes narrowed at me, and I felt the nerves tighten in my belly. He hadn't shaved for a day and the scruff on his jaw looked, dare I say, delicious under the lamplight of the street.

"You have five seconds to sit in the car."

I'll sit wherever you want me to sit, James.

Ignoring the rubbish in my head, I said, "And if I don't?"

"You can walk home, can't you?" He cocked his head to the side.

He wouldn't, would he? I didn't want to bump into another pervert when I walk back home. But he came to my rescue the second I called him and it's a weekend. He could've just called an Uber for me, but he didn't.

Calling his bluff, I scowled at him and raised my chin. "You'd never let me walk home alone at night."

"You're right," he growled, stepping closer and crowding me against the back of his car. He seemed angry before, but now, he looked furious. So furious that he could eat me. "I'd never let you walk home alone, Mia, but I *can* and I *will* let you walk home trailing with my car if you don't put your cute little butt in the car right fucking now."

I don't know why, but I found that extremely hot.

Once again, I was ignoring the rubbish my brain was sprouting out.

He said my butt is cute.

Yep, there was definitely something mixed in my drink.

"I-I want to know what you told that guy."

"Five."

My eyes widened and I pulled his coat closer, getting distracted by his smoky cologne. "You can't do that."

"Four."

"I'm not a kid!"

"Three."

"Are you even listening to me?" I asked, glaring at him.

"Two."

"You know what?" I leaned closer and licked my lips, giving him his coat and thrusting it in his hands. "You can keep this if you want to keep treating me like a child. I'll walk back home on my own."

I turned away from him, walking away.

"*One.*" His smooth voice sent a chill down my spine, "And wrong answer, Princess."

2
YOU'RE HOT

MIA

"And wrong answer, princess."

I swallowed the lump in my throat when he neared me, his tall height looming over me. He seemed so put together, I hated it. Absolutely *loathed* it. I was soaked from my head to toe and my shoes squelched when I moved while he looked untouched from the rain. There I was looking like a wet sock while wearing wet socks, and he looked like he just walked out of an Abercrombie cover shoot.

"W-what are you going to do?" I did not mean to stutter. Stuttering was for the weak, but I'd be lying if I said his closeness didn't affect me. And he smelt so, *so* good. I wanted to bury my nose in his neck and sniff. Even ask about the cologne he used so I could buy it like a little creep and spray it all over my bed and roll around in it.

Yep. There was definitely something in my drinks.

"I'm going to fuck you."

"What?" My lips parted as a car zoomed by and wetness seeped out of me, making my already wet underwear *wetter*.

"You sure... you want to do that?" I looked around the empty walkway, my cheeks feeling warm.

"Of course I'm sure, Mia." He sounded so assertive and stern that it scared and excited me.

It was no surprise that I had the biggest, fastest, and juiciest crush on him since my father introduced him to me a year ago. I was too busy stuffing my food with the wedding cake when he had showed me the fine specimen that was James Fox in a fitted tailored suit. With an awkward, braces-covered, toothy smile and insecure body, I had shyly shaken his hand while he ruffled my hair. *Ruffled.* Like I was a kid to him. Probably was, considering he was eighteen years older than me.

At sixteen, I had filed my attraction towards him in the celebrity crush folder of my brain along with Cillian Murphy, Michael Fassbender, Andrew Garfield, and Tom Hiddleston. I realized that I had a thing for hot older men with British accents, who possibly looked British, too. No biggie, lots of people have crushes on older celebrities, and it took me one look at Tumblr's homepage to notice that.

But my crush on James was anything but simple.

James held my elbow, his grip firm and my skin singed where he touched me, and pointed to the passenger car seat. "*Sit.*"

I craned my neck to look at him and licked my lips when his eyes met mine. "W-what would my father say?"

I almost cringed mentioning him in all of this. I did not want to think about my dad when I was with James, which was very little, but I had to be sure.

If my dad found out his bestfriend slept with his only daughter... *yeah, no, it won't look good.*

He raised a brow, making me scuffle in my shoes. "Your dad doesn't need to know about this." His fingers tightened on my skin as he moved closer, our clothes almost touching. "Now sit in the damn car before I drag you in there."

My dad doesn't need to know?

He *wanted* me to be his dirty little secret.

My tongue felt like lead. I scrambled to the car seat and sat down, trying to calm my heavy breathing, but it wasn't working. All I could think about was his large, veiny hands touching me everywhere, bringing me on the verge of orgasms again and again while he fucked me like he said he would.

"Why are your cheeks red?"

Because I'm having very R-rated thoughts about your hands, tongue, and cock inside me.

"Because I'm cold?" I hid my face behind my hair, hoping he wouldn't notice I now resembled a tomato.

I held my breath when his fingers touched my jaw, making me look at him. His brows were furrowed as his eyes danced over my face, and then he touched my forehead with the back of his palm.

"You're hot."

"Well, I hope so," I replied with an awkward chuckle.

"What did you drink at the party?" he asked, surprising me by leaning closer. I parted my lips to answer, but I got lost in his dreamy eyes. I couldn't muster any thoughts when he was near. *How was I going to be intimate with him when my brain had turned into puddle? Was I even ready for that? With him?* I was pulled back to earth when he pulled the seat belt over me and strapped me in.

Oh. He wasn't going in for a kiss.

Yet.

"I don't remember," I answered, looking down at my lap and cringing at the thought of my wet clothes soaking his expensive leather seat. "I'm sorry for ruining your car seat."

The car started with a smooth purr just by a press of a

button. He flickered his eyes at me and replied, "Don't worry, I get the covers changed every week."

How rich was this guy?

"Why every week?"

His lips curled at the corner. "Because they get stained —*ah*, ruined every week."

I frowned at him. *Ruined by what?*

Shrugging, I leaned back on the comfortable seat and looked out the window, my heart rate increasing with each mile. By the time I noticed the familiar road, I was shivering.

I had to make sure if he really planned to fuck me. Maybe he thought he would give me a start-of-the-high-school-as-a-junior gift by taking my virginity and showing me all the ways of pleasure and desire. He sure looked like sin and I was willing to be his sinner, even on my knees if he asked me to.

But there was one other thing...

"James," I started when he parked the car in my driveway. "I'm seventeen."

He slowly blinked at me. "I know."

Oh, wow, talk about determination.

"I am really seventeen, James," I emphasized. "Like not adult but kind of adult*ish*. I mean, I will be eighteen soon, *haha*, not that it's a problem, but I'm just—"

My eyes lowered to his finger on my lips. My lips burned where the soft padded part of his index finger met the bottom, fuller part of my lips, and all I wanted to do was part my lips and take his finger in. Feel the knuckle of his finger on my tongue and lick it. Taste it. *Suck* it.

"Mia. I know you are seventeen." James pulled away before I could show him my exceptionally amateur sucking skills. I had used those skills once in the back room of Chemistry lab with a classmate, but he came on my expensive new jeans, ruining them, so I never tried it again.

"Come on. Let's go to your bedroom."

I chuckled and ran a hand through my hair. "You don't wait, do you?"

"What's there to wait?"

He unlocked the main door—yes, he even knew the code to our house. That was how much my dad trusted him. *Oh, poor dad. What would he say?* He was with his buddies watching hockey, eating onion rings and thinking his daughter was following the curfew and in bed sound asleep.

"Come on, be quick, Mia. I don't have much time." James ushered me in. "I have early meetings tomorrow."

I'll be in bed for sure. Just for different reasons.

3

LOOK AT ME AND ANSWER

MIA

I swallowed the lump in my throat and stayed by the front door, which he ordered me to do. He came back with a couple of hand towels after rummaging in the washroom closet. I accepted one of them and started patting my hands and tee-shirt, staring in horror at the sight of my nude bra being glaringly visible through the sheer dark top. The only night I decided to wear something sexy and it embarrasses me. *Great, thanks world.*

"Oh," I let out a soft chuckle when he started patting my wet hair with a towel. "You don't have to."

James glared at me. "You'll get sick. You can't miss your first day of school."

"*High* School." I corrected him, crossing my arms.

His eyes lowered to my arms before snapping at my face as heat crept up his neck. "*Junior* year of high school, Mia. You should take a warm shower before bed and take some cold medicine." He touched my forehead again while I shamelessly admired the way his shirt stretched over his shoulders and tightened over his biceps. *He's so hot.* "Your skin is still hot. Come on, let's get you in bed—"

My eyes blinked at his dark mop of thick, soft, very tuggable hair when he knelt in front of me. *What was he doing down there?*

Then I felt his fingers on my shoes as he removed them. I squeaked, "I-I can do that on my own."

James didn't reply. He simply held my leg and peeled off the wet socks. I shivered, holding on to his muscled shoulders when his hand brushed against the soft skin of my feet, tickling me. When he stood up, his pupils were dilated with an emotion I've never seen on his face... or I was possibly dreaming.

I didn't know what he saw on my face, but he shook his head and snapped, "Come on."

He didn't wait for my reply. He held my wrist and dragged me behind him. James didn't realize that he didn't have to tell me twice or take me. I'd follow him wherever he asked me to.

My heart dropped as soon as we entered my room. I had completely forgotten about the mess of clothes, shoes, makeup, and underwear that I had created while getting ready for the party and leaving it 'for later' before I rushed out.

"Bite my ass," I muttered underneath my breath and shoved the clothes in my closet, almost tripping on a pair of black stilettos. I grunted and heaved, trying to clear my queen-sized princess bed as much as I could.

James must look at my room and think how immature I was. With Korean band posters I outgrew, a *Speed* movie poster because I loved Keanu Reeves, and small polaroids of me and my friends stuck all around the light peach-colored walls.

"I'm sorry." I blushed when he helped me gently remove the band of cherry red push-up bra that was too tiny for my girlies from the corner of the door. "I don't know how it got up there."

"You don't have to apologize. When I was your age, my room looked like an after scene from a war zone."

I bit my lip and nodded, throwing the bra in my dresser and slamming it shut. "So how do you... how do you want to do this?" I asked, looking at my bed with its pink floral duvet cover, nine pillows and two stuffed toys.

I was about to get railed by my crush, who is my father's best-friend slash my soon-to-be-hot-teacher, on the same princess bed he had helped my dad install.

Talk about mid-teen-life-crush crisis.

"Take a shower first."

"*Oh*," I straightened up. I didn't think I smelt that bad, but... okay. "I'll be right—"

A shrill ringtone broke our eye contact. I ignored the tug in my heart when he picked up the call. I could hear a woman's voice on the other end and my heart dropped a little more.

When he ended the call, I knew what he was going to say, so I kept my fake smile ready.

"I'm sorry, Mia. I've to leave soon."

"Of course." I smiled big and wide, nodding way too fast. "No problem."

James walked towards me and I held my breath when his lips came closer and landed on my forehead. "Don't forget to take a hot shower before you tuck yourself in, okay?"

"Of course, James. I'm a big girl now." My smile froze, and I repeated his words in my head. "Wait, what did you just say?"

"I said don't forget to take a hot shower."

"No, after that."

"Tuck yourself in?"

I stared at him and blinked. "You… you wanted to tuck me in?"

"Yes. I said I'm going to tuck you, before we arrived home." He frowned at me and tilted his head. "Are you sure you are okay?"

James never said he wanted to fuck me. He wanted to *tuck* me.

Oh my god, you stupid fucking fool.

"Haha. You wanted to tuck me. *Haha.* Of course. Classic *tuck*ing in. *Ha.*"

"You know what?" He pulled out his phone. "On a second note, you don't seem fine. I'll sleep on the couch."

I stopped him from typing out a text to the woman he was going to meet after *tuck*ing me in. I threw cold water on the jealousy that climbed up my heart that wanted him to stay the night, and forced out the awkward words, "It's okay. I'm okay. I'll take a shower and sleep. *Tuck*ing myself."

"Are you sure you don't want me to stay?"

Of course, I want you to stay! I want you to stay with me and gently pat my hair dry after I take a warm shower. I want you to stay and cuddle with me under my floral covers and tell me a story like my mother used to before she passed away. I want you to stay by my side because I'm selfish, and never let you go to warm someone else's bed because I hate it when I'm alone in this damn big house. I want you to stay and wrap your arms around me and tell me it's going to be okay even when it's not going to be.

"Yes, I'm okay!" I smiled and turned around to find my robe so I could shut myself in the shower and he wouldn't have to see the warm tears burning my eyes.

I bit my lip from spilling out my heart when he held up my hand and brushed his lips against my knuckles. The soft touch of his velvety lips sent shivers down my spine, my stomach tightening with nerves as his warm hand cradled mine.

"Call me if you feel sick, okay?"

I nodded, not meeting his eyes because it hurt to see him leave.

His hold tightened on my hand. "Look at me and answer."

"I'll call you if I get sick." I rolled my eyes and met his piercing blue eyes. "Happy now?"

His eyes narrowed at me. "I don't like that tone, young lady. I'm older than you."

"So? You're like eighteen years older. It doesn't matter."

He said underneath his breath, but I caught it, "You don't have to remind me."

Before I could ask what he meant by that, he squeezed my hand and pulled away. "Goodnight, Mia."

I watched his back disappear out of the hallway, going downstairs as I whispered to an empty room, "Goodnight, James."

James

I relaxed my fingers from a tight fist and stared at it.

Soft. Sweet. Innocent.

And your friend's seventeen-year-old daughter.

Shaking my head, I closed my eyes and erased all impure thoughts about a certain doe-eyed vixen with soaking clothes. But it didn't help. Her cherry-scented perfume was all over in the car, and I fucking hated myself for wanting that perfume in every nook and cranny of my car, my clothes, my skin.

"*Hell*," I said to myself, glaring at the two-story house where my sin lived. "You're going to hell for your thoughts, James."

I sighed and messaged her dad and my close friend, Clyde

Miller, that his daughter was home safe before shutting down my phone. I had a long night, and I intended to lash out everything on the red-haired woman that had called me.

I would need it. Especially if I was going to torture myself for the next year by teaching a bunch of highschoolers.

4
PORN STAR NAME

MIA

Waking up with soaked underwear was not ideal. Especially when the reason for the particular soaked underwear was my father's bestfriend, James Fox.

Yes, even his name sounds like a porn star.

Biting my lip, I turned on my back and took a deep breath. I could try it again. Surely, it would be easy after trying to touch myself so many times. Maybe too easy.

You can do it, Mia. Just think about his handsome face, his delicious stern voice, his dark hair and—*fuck, yes, mmm.*

My hands felt small and gentle, cupping my perky breasts. I imagined his large palms—with the *Patek Philippe* on his wrist that I had gifted him on his thirty-fifth birthday—fondling my breasts, the veins on his forearms tensing as he pinches my hard little nipples between his fingers.

A whimper tore out of my lips as my thighs rubbed together, my pussy getting wetter and wetter when I thought about him instructing me how to touch my pussy.

Nonono, in my dream, he calls it *his pussy*.

Yes, *his* pussy. My feminist self really yeets out whenever I have horny thoughts about him.

My eyes flickered to the side, watching my reflection on the closet mirror. My cheeks were flushed, eyes clouded with lust, my palms touching my naked breasts and lowering over my stomach. Caressing the smooth skin and shivering at the image of James in my head.

I parted my legs like he would, keeping his strong hand over my thigh and peeling off my satin shorts with my soaked underwear, mocking me for ruining them with my juices. Oh, how deliciously wicked he'd look with that dark look in his eyes. Even forcing the underwear in my willing mouth when he would go down on me and make me cum with his hot tongue.

Letting out a small moan, I slid my hand inside my underwear, humming when the pad of my finger made contact with my aching clit. The sensitive nub was swollen and buzzing with pleasure as I rubbed it slowly, thinking about his encouraging words in his deep, husky voice.

Just like that, Mia.

That's it.

That's how good girls touch their cunts.

No, no, no, keep going, I didn't tell you to stop.

You are going to cream all over your little fingers for me, hm?

"Mia!"

All my fantasies came crashing down upon hearing the booming voice in the hallway. I removed my hand from my underwear and sat up straight, finding my satin shirt on the floor, which I had discarded last night before sleeping.

No matter what the internet tells you, sleeping naked is a blessing for your body. Especially your breasts.

"Mia, you will be late." My father knocked on the door, making all my fantasies about his best friend vanish.

Taming my hair, I straightened my clothes and opened

the door to show him my charming smile. "I won't be late," I said in a cheesy voice, but it seemed too high-pitched. "I will be out of the room in twenty minutes."

"You better, kiddo, if you want me to drop you off. I have an early meeting today."

"Ay, ay, captain!" I closed the door and sighed after locking myself in the bathroom. My cheeks were still flushed and my heart was hammering against my ribs.

If only no one had interrupted me… maybe, just maybe, I would finally know what an orgasm felt like.

"No time to think about it," I muttered to myself and stripped out of my clothes and got in the shower.

I shaved, shampooed and conditioned my shoulder-length hair, and brushed my teeth in the record time of fifteen minutes. I was lucky enough to be enrolled in a private school, so we had to wear a uniform. Crisp white shirt paired with green and black plaid skirt and white socks with shoes of our preference. I altered between my chunky Doc Martens and Mary Janes. Being the first day of my junior year, I opted for Mary Janes.

I wore my favorite jewelry, a dainty heart necklace, and placed it under my shirt. My mom had gifted it to me on the night she died.

Hanging the tie over my shoulder, I ran downstairs with my small backpack in hand and thanking my father for the breakfast.

"Are you ready for the new year, Pumpkin?" he asked, taking the tie from me and expertly tying it for me and handing it back. It was our ritual as I could not, for the life of me, learn how to tie a tie or tie shoelaces. He had tried to teach me, but it was fruitless.

"I am ready, but a little nervous," I answered, eating the strawberries after devouring the eggs. "I have a lot of AP classes and I don't want to fail in any of them."

"You won't," he said and smiled at me. "Even if you do, you know I don't care. Just stay sane and healthy, Pumpkin."

"Yes, Captain."

I applied a little concealer, mascara and lip gloss in the mirror by the hall where mom used to keep her makeup and her little jewelries before going out. I smiled sadly at the picture frame of her by Dad's bedroom that used to be their room before an accident took her away from us.

His arm wrapped around my shoulder and I closed my eyes, breathing in the cozy scent of pumpkin and wood with a lingering whiff of her perfume. I knew he would spritz it on himself, trying to imagine having her back in his arms.

He kissed my head. "She would be very proud to see you today, Mia."

"What?" I chuckled. "Almost late for school?"

He ruffled my hair, and I frowned at him, running my hand through my damp hair and following him into the garage. "You don't have to be nervous. James will be there."

That's the fucking problem, Dad.

"And I told him to take care of you, so you don't have to worry about anything, but maintaining your—"

"Sanity." I ended the sentence for him and closed the car door of the passenger seat. "By the way, Dad… when am I getting my own car again?"

He turned on the ignition of the car and rolled it out of the garage. "When you behave well."

"Which I do."

"*Hmm.*"

"Don't *hmm* me." I sulked in my seat and crossed my arms. "I would love to drive with my friends and go—"

"*Mia.*" He glanced at me, his salt and pepper hair styled the same way since my childhood, his brown eyes stern with lines around them. "If you want to earn a car, you have to show me that you will be responsible for it."

"By doing what, exactly?" I was vexed. "I worked in the diner for three summer vacations and saved up for it, and now you are telling me to be responsible for it. *How?*"

He, of course, didn't reply. I groaned and looked out of the window, wishing Mom was alive and would let me have a car. It wasn't like I couldn't just go in a car shop and buy it since I would become an adult soon, but he was my father, the only person who I was really close to, and I didn't want to do anything without his support.

Or cause him any disappointment.

I looked at the expensive cars that lined up outside the Saint Helena Academy. Sons and daughters of actors, models, and businessmen getting dropped off by the intimidating tall gates. The academy was built on the grounds of the old Saint Helena Palace, with a church on the academic grounds. It was in shambles until a rich billionaire restored the palace and turned it into a private academy for rich kids.

"Have a great day, Pumpkin. Love you!" My father yelled at me as soon as I opened the door and got out, scowling at him.

I quickly showed him my back and walked through the gates, eyeing the intimidating, looming towers of the school. It even had freaking turrets. The palace had three official buildings, and each had their own division for the students and teachers—one for junior high, the biggest one for senior high, and the other one for teachers that also held a gym, an ice rink, and a pool for our sports classes. There was rumored to be an old church somewhere in the trees behind the teachers' building, but it was supposed to be haunted and securities lurked around it as it was off grounds for everyone.

I didn't have a thing for haunted churches in the forest, but my curiosity for it burned me.

My eyes flickered to the vast parking lot where more

luxurious, shiny cars were parked with assigned spots for teachers, and students whose parents donated a large sum to keep the academy running.

"Funny to see you alive and sulking on this fine morning, Mia!" I greeted my friend, Summer Hayes, with a grin as she wrapped her arm around me and walked with me to the hallway. "I finished the entire fantasy series last night, and the descriptions of his dong were just chef's kiss."

"You did not just say dong out loud."

"*Dong.*" Summer grinned, "See? I did it again. Oh, look, there's Emma. I will scare her."

I giggled when she ran over to Emma, hugging her from behind and screaming dong in her ear. The poor girl squeaked, making the other people laugh around her for messing with her.

"I hate you," Emma grumbled, rubbing her ear and fixing her beige cardigan. "You are annoying."

Summer poked her tongue out at her. "If you truly hate me, then I won't share the delicious Thai curry my mom cooked for us."

"Summer, you shouldn't yell dong out loud in the hallways or a teacher will scold us." I shuddered, thinking about getting a detention ticket for that. "Or even suspend us. Did you hear what happened to Thomas last year?"

"He skinny dipped in the school pool and Ms. Laxmi found him. Big deal." Emma said as we leaned against her locker, her pastel-colored nails matching her lilac pink purse and the bow pinned on her hair. Her locker was filled with pictures of the three of us, and her and her boyfriend.

"I have heard there's a new faculty joining us this year."

I looked away and found my locker, stashing my books in it and checking my course list again. I did not want to get involved in the talk of James Fox and—

"Yeah, the dude's name is James Fox," Summer said. "It's such a porn star name. Sounds sus, if you ask me."

You and me both.

"Summer." I elbowed her and nodded at Ms. Laxmi, who was walking past us, checking if the students of Saint Helena academy were behaving or not. "You are asking—*no*, begging for a detention slip. Do you want a mic?"

"*Girl*," she drawled out, sighing and clutching one of her fantasy books in her arms as she went off to la-la land, "The only begging I will do is for his perfectly sized twelve inch do—*semester!*"

She yelled out and straightened up when the dean of our academy gave her a pointed look. I suppressed a shudder when her dark eyes slid to me and Emma. She kept her chin high until she walked away, disappearing between other students.

"Whew, that was close."

I deadpanned, "You think? She will expel you without any thoughts if she had heard you."

She rolled her eyes at me. "Come on, we can't even talk about our fantasies out loud?"

"Sexual fantasies, Summer."

"So? If my mom paid a bit more of a donation, she would forget she ever heard me." She flashed me her teeth and pulled out her notes for the subject.

The bell rang, followed shortly by asking the students to visit the auditorium hall for the first day and get inspired to study more. It was a given that most of us would go to Ivy League universities as soon as we graduate from Saint Helena academy, and get high paying jobs just seeing the name of the academy in our CV.

My mother wanted me to study here and if it wasn't for her, I wouldn't have joined the academy last year... so soon after she died. In a way, I had to thank James and my father for helping me pass the entrance exam for the academy, and fit right in with Emma and Summer.

"We hope you will achieve all your dreams from the Saint Helena academy and let us help you create a better future." The dean ended her speech with a stern voice, eyeing all of us through her sharp glasses.

"My dream is to get fucked by six vampires—"

I elbowed Summer, and held my breath when her eyes slid to our group, glaring directly at Summer, who met her levelling stare.

"See me after your last class, Miss Summer Hayes."

Everyone looked at her, some people chuckling and glaring at her, and a boy outright making an expression of slicing his throat before turning away.

"Don't worry," I said to her when she left the podium. "I will cry on your funereal and play Taylor Swift's songs."

"Har har," she said, flicking her hair over her shoulder. "What's the worst she can do? *Nothing*. I am Summer fucking Hayes."

"Let's go, Mia." Emma wrapped her arm around my elbow. "Summer is still thinking about her five vampire lords and getting railed by them."

"Six vampire lords, Em! *Six*," Summer corrected with a grin. "Keep up!"

I laughed with her and waved at Summer, who had a class in the east wing of the Palace-slash-academy. I wondered why I hadn't seen James during the main assembly. Maybe he was teaching some other class or maybe he would join the next year.

That would be much better. I didn't want to go through the torture of sitting through his lectures, hearing his melodious deep voice and my pussy aching for him. Only if my friends knew how not-so innocent I was, pretending to be a goody two shoes when all I wanted was my father's friend to wrap his hand around my neck and thrust inside me.

Yes. It would be a blessing in disguise if he wouldn't have a class this semester.

But of course, why would God ever listen to a white seventeen-year-old who had sex dreams about her dad's best friend?

"Good morning," James said, prowling into my third class as if he owned the entire building. "I am James Fox and your teacher for Design and Colors."

Oh goodie, this was not good for me or my underwear.

5

YES, MISTER JAMES?

MIA

His voice rang through the class of twenty teenagers, grabbing our attention and making me squirm in my seat. I tugged at the tie that felt too tight around my neck, trying not to ogle at his tall, broad-shouldered frame. He looked delicious in a fitted crisp white shirt and pants. His shoes were so shiny I wondered if he took an extra hour to polish them. Nah, must have gotten someone else to do it.

But what stood out the most were his glasses. Black frame that perched on his strong nose as his eyes glimmered through them, making me squirm in my seat.

I swallowed the lump in my throat when he answered a small question from a girl, rolling the sleeves of his shirt over his elbow. *Fuck, his arms.* His hands. The watch that I had gifted him glinted in the light streaming in through the open windows.

"Why does his name sound like a porn star?" a guy behind me whispered, and I had to bite the insides of my cheek to stop myself from laughing.

Thank god, I wasn't the only one.

"Is there something you want to share with the class, Matt?" I straightened up, hearing James address the guy behind me. His delicious voice sent shivers down my body, and I had to clench my thighs to suppress myself from looking at him.

"N-no, sir, just surprised to have a new teach for such a small subject."

Uh-oh, he had a death wish.

James chuckled, and I glanced at him when he straightened to his full height, walking out from behind the desk, leaning back on it. He stretched out his long legs in front of him, addressing the class.

"Matt, what do you want to get out of graduating from Saint Helena academy?"

His answer was quick. "I want to get into an Ivy League university, get a degree, maybe get my master's degree and get a job that makes me rich with a big house and a hot girlfriend—"

"I'll stop you right there." Our teacher smiled, students snickering with him. "Who else wants to get rich and live in a big house as Matt put it?"

Everyone raised their arms. Everyone except one. I rolled my eyes when he pointed out Emma.

"And your reason miss…"

"Emma," she answered, crossing her arms and leaning back on the chair. "I already live in a mansion and I don't need to get rich, Mister Fox. I *am* rich."

"Of course," he pursed his lips and got back on the topic. "As most of you want to get rich, earn a lot of money, you will also either buy or build luxurious houses, apartments or buildings for your clients. But before that, you need to learn how space and design works."

"That sounds so boring."

He nodded at the girl who said it, "It does, but in the

future you will thank me for teaching you how to design. So stop whining and look over the material I hand you."

I leaned down to take out my notes from my backpack when I heard his voice—much closer to me, startling me out of the stupor from his introduction.

"Miss Miller?"

My heartbeat stuttered as I eyed his polished shoes and my eyes drifted over his perfectly ironed slacks, his belt, the buttons of his shirt, his delectable adam's-apple, the scruff on his sharp jaw, kissable lips, and strong nose to his dark green eyes.

"Y-yes?" I asked, blinking at him. "Yes, Mister James?"

"Can you share these notes with your classmates?"

I'll do anything you ask me to if you keep looking at me like that.

He kept a bundle of spiral notes on my desk, but I was too busy ogling the short lock of hair that was falling right over his left brow, making him look much more desirable. I wanted to lean closer and tuck it away.

Clearing my throat, I stood up, my chair squeaking behind me as I held the notes closer and nodded quickly, avoiding his eyes but memorizing his bare forearm—*ohmygod he has veins on his hands and arms*—and turned around to hand over the notes before I lean closer to him in front of all my classmates.

That would be a pretty embarrassing thing to do on the first day of school.

I can do that on the last day of school.

MIA, GET YOUR HEAD OUT OF THE GUTTER—

"Is there some problem, Miss Miller?"

Yes, you see I have been getting wet dreams about you for a while, and you were the reason I was being so squirmy right now because my panties were soaked just hearing you say a few things about the class, wearing THOSE pants that make your ass looks so... *delectable*.

Holding back my shiver, I continued sharing the notes and smiled at him, "No problem, Sir."

James

Just one look at her flushed cheeks and glazed hazel-green eyes, I knew what dirty little Mia was thinking about that made her squirm every few seconds on her chair. It was distracting to see her cross and uncross her legs with her plaid skirt lowering on her thigh. It made me clench my fingers in a fist from scolding her, because her male classmates couldn't keep their eyes from the revealing skin.

But I had promised to be a good teacher, a better friend to Clyde, and signed the contract, so insistent on teaching young minds the art of design.

No matter how jealous I was, no matter how tempting the distraction was, no matter how my hands were itching to slip under her skirt, and scold her for ruining her underwear—it was *wrong*.

She was seventeen years old, and even worse, my friend's daughter.

Clyde Miller was one of my first clients when I had joined the world of design as an intern. He must have seen potential in me. That was the only reason he helped me, even loaned me money out of his own pocket when I couldn't afford to buy anything else than eggs or rice. Not to mention he was stubbornly kind towards me since that night.

So I had made the wise decision of sticking to teaching and focusing on answering the questions students had. Even when she raised her hand, tucking a dark stray lock behind her ear and asked me about the three-point-perspective in her sweet voice.

Thankfully, the bell rang announcing the period was over, and it was amusing to see how everyone started packing their bags, boys bumping my fists as if I was one of them, before walking out of the class and hooting.

Ah, reminds me how loud I was as a teenager.

"Miss Miller," I called her as she walked past my desk with her friend, who narrowed her eyes at me. She came from old money. I could tell from one look at her, but I couldn't give a shit. "I thought you already knew about all three perspectives."

Mia's eyes widened a little before she faced me with an innocent expression on her face, her notes in her hands. "I know, but I wanted to test you, Mister Fox. Hope you have a wonderful first day at Saint Helena Academy."

I kept my eyes on her as she walked away with her friend, laughing about something and leaving me alone in the class with a pang of arousal and guilt.

Closing my eyes, I took a deep breath and erased the filthy, corrupting thoughts from my head. They were just that, *thoughts*.

Empty desires and nothing more.

I got a ping on my phone and checked the message. I exhaled sharply, seeing a text from Clyde Miller.

Clyde: Good luck on your first day of teaching! As Mia would say, 'Go and get some.'

Me: Thank you, but for the love of God, please never ever repeat—or type that sentence again.

Clyde: Yeet

Me: -_-

Clyde: XD Gottem

Me: I have a couple more classes, so see you around, old man.

Clyde: Ay, don't forget about today's dinner!

My brows furrowed, and I had to check my calendar's

app to see that I had blocked my evening with 'Dinner @ Miller's House - Gift' from four to eight in the evening.

Shit, I have to get the gifts, too.

Having dinner with them every other week or every month had started since I met Clyde, but I had avoided going to his house. It stopped briefly over a few years when I went abroad to further my knowledge about Green engineering and working on a few projects, but we had started our dinner rituals again since last year. I'd either visit them or they would visit my house. Gifting was optional, but we gladly appreciated alcohol and books with some sort of dessert, as both Clyde and his daughter had an extremely sweet tooth.

My phone vibrated in my hand, and I glanced at the upcoming message from him.

Clyde: By the lack of your response, either your class has started, or you forgot about the dinner.

Me: I didn't exactly forget about it. I'll be there, don't worry.

After all, I have never missed a single dinner or lunch with them.

* * *

THE FIRST DAY of school ended with a small email from the dean, who wanted to make sure we were all on our best behaviors and showing enthusiasm for the year.

As much as I had fun teaching students about design, space, and colors, I missed being in my private office. The solitude and quietness that came with drafting on sheets, the rough but comfortable sound of lead pencil drifting through the paper, and my loud head brimming with ideas to turn the dream of my clients into a reality.

But I was teaching, sharing my secrets with young minds,

and I knew it would help them in their future. I just had to teach until the contract ends.

Packing my notes in the briefcase, I closed the lights in the office that the school had offered me. It was a comfortable room with a couch, desk and chairs, bookshelves, a little storage room and even a bathroom. Considering it was a private academy, no wonder they offered such luxuries to teachers as well, with their high pay.

I remembered my public school and how tiny the teachers' office was, and they didn't have their own office or an entire building to themselves. You'd have to go to the ground floor and hope that the teacher wasn't busy to help you with your doubts.

"James."

I paused and looked at the dark hair of the familiar figure. Removing my black-framed glasses, I stood beside her. "What are you doing here, Mia?"

From what I knew after the teacher's orientation, students rarely crossed over to the teachers' building unless it was really important. My eyes zeroed in on her face, her arms and legs. Not noticing any bruise, I tilted my head, "Are you in trouble?"

6

STUDIES AND CHILL

JAMES

"Are you in trouble?"

"Of course, you'd think I'm here because I'm in trouble." She scoffed, rolling her eyes at me, and I ignored the itch to do something completely irrational and uncivilized. "Mister Steven asked me to assist him after class."

Steven? The Math teacher. He had grey hair and looked like the sweet grandpa who snuck a few sugar candies to you when your mom wasn't looking.

I fell in step beside her, our footsteps echoing in the empty hallway. "I didn't know students could assist teachers."

"I only help him because he gives chocolates. Look, James." She pulled out two dark toffees in a bright wrapper from her skirt. Her eyes were dancing with a gleam of joy and it made me happy to see her like that.

"Why don't you address me properly as your teacher?"

I didn't mean to ask her such a question in a dark tone. My mouth ran before my brain did.

Her hazel eyes roved over my figure, and I felt an odd

tightness as she licked her lips and looked away. "Do you really want me to call you Mister James?"

Yes. No. This is a terrible idea.

Being alone with her. Standing so close that I can smell her cherry perfume again.

I looked at the grey clouds and echoing thunder. It would rain soon. I could smell it in the thick air. There were very few cars left in the parking lot, and I didn't know how she was going to get home.

"Is Clyde going to pick you up?"

She walked with me to the common grounds of the palace where all the three buildings met under an overarching hallway covered by thick pillars and grass. I bit my cheek from smiling at seeing the wallpaper on her phone screen when she unlocked it.

Last month, we all had made a bet playing Monopoly, and she lost against me and Clyde, going bankrupt, so she had to put an awkward picture of her as a wallpaper. She was being a dork with tousled hair and poking her tongue at the camera. It was cute, but she had complained that she hated that picture.

"No, my friend usually drops me, or I walk but—"

"Are you waiting for someone?" I raised my brow, glancing at my watch. "Your boyfriend?" My voice sounded different. Too deep and low.

Mia laughed, my eyes meeting hers, noting how she barely reached my shoulder. "A boyfriend? Seriously, James? Do you think I, of all people, would have a boyfriend?"

I scratched my neck and didn't reply. I didn't want to know about her love life as long as she was being safe.

"Mia!"

I looked over at Miss Moore, Emma, embracing Mia in a hug. Her cheeks were flushed as if she had run to meet her.

"Mister James, you're still in school?"

I ignored her question and looked at her and the boy who was walking past us towards the shiny red sports car. I was sure I had seen his face somewhere.

"I believe there is time and place for whatever you were doing, but a school classroom is not one of them, Miss Moore," I said and nodded at Mia. "Goodbye, Mia."

The two teens started whispering in hushed voices while I walked away. I couldn't care less what they did in the classroom, but I hoped Mia wasn't following in the footsteps of her friend. I know I had no say in what she did—or *who* she did, but I wanted her to be safe. Especially from jerks of her age who would promise anything to get in her pants.

Fuck. I have no right to think or act like her dad.

I sighed, seeing the silhouette of Mia running towards me when rain started pattering. She quickly opened the door of the passenger seat and made herself at home in my car.

"Comfortable enough?" I deadpanned.

"Oh, yes, thank you very much." She ended her call and smiled at me. "Dad said you are joining us for dinner, so if you don't mind, would you be so kind to drop me home? Please?"

She didn't need to tell me twice. Her smile was enough to make me do anything she wanted. Which was a curse and a blessing.

"Of course, Princess." I started the engine of the car and rolled out of the spot when it purred to life. I watched her friend get into the red car of the boy from before. "What happened to your friend who was going to drop you?"

Mia shook her head, fixing her seatbelt, and I forced my eyes above her neck. Her white shirt had gotten wet from the rain. I didn't have an extra jacket or a blanket in the car to give her.

"She is going to his house for studies."

"Is that the new slang you use?"

"Slang?"

"Yes, like Netflix and chill. Studies and chill?"

Mia's soft chuckle echoed in the car as rain continued to patter outside as I slowly drove us to her house.

"You are such a dork, James," she snickered, wiping her eyes. "They are dating, but he is going to help her study."

I hummed and flickered my eyes at her. Her mascara was a little smudged on the corner of her eyes, a few strays of her hair were wet and her cheeks were flushed with a rosy tint. As if she had just basked in the heat of the Italian summer.

"You didn't answer my question," I asked her when the white manor came into the view.

"What question?"

"Do you have a boyfriend?"

"I don't... I don't have a boyfriend, James." Her voice was soft, too soft, and her lips were too invi—

"Good girl."

Mia glanced at me when I took a turn, her eyes wide.

"Y-you didn't answer my question either..." Her cheeks were warm, too warm and flushed, with her bottom lip trapped between her teeth. All too sudden, she was everywhere as rain continued to storm outside. Her cherry flavored perfume, her glazed green eyes, dilated pupils that made me want to yank off the seatbelts and sin.

I had to force my eyes from her wet bottom lip when she whispered in the quiet of my car, "Do you want me to address you as Mister James?"

7
I WILL REWARD YOU

MIA

"Do you want me to address you as Mister James?"

I didn't know what came over me to ask that question, but I wanted to know. I've addressed him as James since we've met, and I enjoyed calling him by his first name. Would he like that? Me addressing him as one of his students?

His blue eyes flickered to me. The shadows from the car and the rainy weather made them seemed dark, almost black. I clasped my hands together in my lap, feeling the dampness of my skirt, and squirmed under his heated gaze. It burned me.

His eyes noticed the movement, and I held my breath, waiting for his answer. He looked back at the road and answered in a low, gruff voice, "Call me whatever you want, Mia."

"Whatever I want?"

He didn't reply.

I pressed. "I'll call you James. But in school, I'll call you Mister James."

He still didn't reply. I wanted to look at his face and try to find out what he was thinking, but he didn't turn to face me. Instead, he kept driving, his knuckles turning white from their grip on the steering wheel.

Feeling dejected, I looked away and slouched on the same seat that I had been in less than twenty-four hours. I made tiny circles on my thigh with my finger and thought about the homework and assignments that I had to finish before going to bed. Sighing, I was about to get comfortable in the seat when I noticed the streets.

James wasn't driving me home.

My stomach dipped. "Where are we going? My home is the other way."

"Change of plans." He shifted the gear, and out of habit, my eyes drifted to his arms. I licked my lips and removed my gaze from the veins. I knew he was in a great shape. Anyone could notice that by the way he filled out all his clothes with his broad shoulders and tapered waist. But he wasn't muscular like the jocks from my school. He was lean, tall and his forearms had delicious veins whenever he clenched his hands. I liked it. I liked it a lot.

Feeling the dampness in my underwear, I shifted and focused on his words. I was bad, bad. Crushing on my dad's bestfriend wasn't enough. Now I was crushing on my hot teacher too.

"Did you hear me, Mia?"

Feeling like a deer caught in headlights, I pursed my lips and nodded. I hadn't realized he had already parked us in the underground parking lot of one of the most famous shopping malls in Coral Springs.

"Really?" James tilted his head. "What did I say?"

I bit my lip and blurted whatever came to my head. "That you are rewarding me for my excellence?"

His brows raised, and I hated and loved how frozen I

became under his penetrating gaze, pinning me to the seat. "What excellence, Princess?"

My skin warmed hearing his nickname for me.

"My excellence at surviving the first day of junior year?"

"Mhmm," he hummed, his eyes lit with humor. "Come on, I'll reward you with anything you want."

Anything? I wanted to press. *Even touching me, kissing me, making love to me on my princess bed while I moan your name and beg you to cuddle with me afterwards?*

"Yes, sir!" I beamed, leaving my school backpack in the car and following him on the way to the mall. I didn't miss the way his eyes gleamed upon hearing my words. I wondered what he was thinking.

An hour later, after visiting a few shops, James' strong hands were holding a few bags that included gifts wrapped with bows. I had whined, pouted and complained to him when he wouldn't let me see them and ordered me to go visit other stores while he bought them. I had agreed, even though I wanted to sneak a peek at what he was buying. Only because giving small gifts to each other during weekly dinner was a tradition I had vowed to follow forever.

"I don't know how Clyde deals with you," he said with a stern face, eyeing me as I licked my third cone of ice cream. "You're an insolent child."

Hating that he thought of me as nothing but a child, I shrugged, masking my features and focusing on the sweet goodness of strawberry. "You told me to get anything I want. I wanted three ice creams. You can't call me an insolent child for that."

Before he could reply, I walked off to the big pink neon sign of one of my favourite shops that displayed mannequins in cute pastel dresses. "I need to go in there. They barely have a sale like this!" I was almost licking the glass of the shopping window and eyeing the lilac purple dress. It had a square neckline and reached mid-thigh. The material looked expensive and my hands were itching to touch it.

"Finish your ice cream first."

James didn't have to tell me twice as I gobbled it up in a few seconds and marched into the store, ignoring the shake of his head. I oohed, ahhed and awwed at all the bikinis, dresses, tops and bottoms. They even had footwear, and I was drooling over a certain pair of white sandal heels that looked like heeled Mary Janes.

Case in point, I was in love.

"Aren't you going to buy anything?" James asked, picking up a blouse, looking confused as he rubbed his fingers through the material.

I heard the two teenagers swoon over my back and I looked down at myself, my clothes. Everyone in the store had been staring at him as soon as he entered. His tall, looming height and his handsome face weren't hard to miss among the crowd. While he looked perfect in a shirt rolled over his elbows, pants and polished boots, I looked like a mess in my uniform. My white school shirt was rumpled, the tie was loose around the neck and my boots looked dirty from running around all day.

I put down the floral bikini. "No. Let's go home."

I couldn't stand one more jealous stare at my back or I was sure I was going to burn up.

He glanced at my face and put down the blouse and walked towards me. I swallowed the lump in my throat and took a step back when he kept getting closer, invading my space. I was about to ask what he was doing when he leaned over and picked the bikini I was looking at from the rack.

"This is cute," he said, eyes drifting over the two-piece string light pink bikini with red little cherries on them. "You should get this."

Heat bloomed on my face as I tucked my hair behind my ear. "I can't."

He frowned. "Why not?"

"I didn't bring my wallet. It's in the bag and bag is—what are you doing?"

I followed him when he started walking, holding the hanger that held the bikini. "I said I will reward you, Princess."

My eyes widened as he stopped before the changing rooms and handed me the bikini and the lilac purple dress from before. He tilted his head to one of the rooms and said, "Go try them on."

My stomach churned, but I accepted the clothes from him, too nervous to say anything. I went into the first changing room, closing the curtain behind me, and blinked at my reflection in the mirror. My entire face and neck were flushed.

"It doesn't mean anything," I whispered to myself, stripping out of my uniform and putting on the dress.

It looked better than I thought it would and I couldn't stop playing with its soft but expensive fabric. I had to remove my bra because the chest size was perfect for my girlies and I didn't want to suffocate them. I couldn't reach for the zipper and my cheeks flushed harder, knowing I had to ask James to zip it up.

It doesn't mean anything.

"James," I called out, poking my head through the curtain to find him leaning on the wall with crossed arms. *Yummy.* "Can you help me zip up?"

PART II

"See me after class."

8
IT DOESN'T MEAN ANYTHING

MIA

I parted the curtain when he prowled towards me, and I felt small against him. Standing barefoot in just a little cute dress. Licking my lips, I turned around and felt his warm presence on my back. The hairs on the back of my nape rose up when he took a step closer.

I watched him in the mirror reflection, the delicious clench of his jaw as his fingers moved my hair over my shoulder. I shivered at the brush of his electrifying touch and fidgeted with my hands in front of me. His hot breath brushed against my bare shoulder as he made a low voice from his throat.

"What happened?" My voice was barely audible because that sound. *That sound.* It did things to me that weren't appropriate one bit.

His ocean eyes met mine through the reflection. "You're not wearing a bra."

Oh. *Oh.*

The sound of zipper filled around us and it felt like we were in our own cocoon with no one around. I liked it. I liked it very much. I hated that I liked it very much.

"Were you braless the entire day, Princess?" his deep voice whispered in my ear, goosebumps raking through my body hearing his gruff voice with such intimacy.

I squirmed on my feet, trying to ease off the burning and rubbing my thighs together. His eyes darkened when he stayed rooted behind me even after zipping the dress. "I—*of course not. The dress was a little tight,*" I explained, looking at him.

Big mistake.

I hadn't counted the math in my head because we were hair's breadth away from each other. His eyes, his face, his lips were too close, and I was finding it hard to breathe. The pupils of his eyes dilated when he whispered, his warm large hand still on my back, "Good."

He took a step back and turned me around so he could have a look. All too sudden, I didn't want this dress for me. I wanted it for him. So he could look at me like that again and again. He tilted his head, a frown between his brows. "You need heels."

Before I could utter a single word, he gave me a pair of the white heeled Mary Janes that I had seen before. The heel was over four inches but thankfully it had a strap on the ankle.

"Wear them."

I nodded, my tongue heavy in my mouth, and leaned down. I started hearing that sound from his throat again. It almost resembled a groan... or a growl. I couldn't really tell.

"Stay still," he said to me, his eyes dark when I straightened up. I frowned when he knelt down in front of me. He kept one of the heels on his thigh and looked at me.

I blushed harder and holding his shoulder, I put on the heels. His deft fingers strapped the buckle and moved to the other foot. I watched his hand linger on my ankle as his eyes slowly slid up the length of my leg.

Between them.

"James…" I scrunched my hand on the fabric of his shirt and felt his shoulders tense when he noticed something.

"You're wet," he whispered, more to himself than me. When I tried to move my leg at the embarrassment, he tightened his hold on my ankle. His eyes were pinned on the spot between my legs. "You've soaked your panties, Princess."

"James, I…"

He looked at me and I took a sharp breath, seeing the sharp, wicked look on his face. He looked different. He wasn't sad, angry, or happy. No, I had never seen this look on his face until then. It scared me. It excited me.

"*Please.*"

I didn't know the word was out of my mouth until it was too late. I didn't know why I had said that. I didn't know what I was saying please for.

His hand inched higher on my calf and I was shivering. "Please what?" he asked, his finger rubbing the soft part on the back of my knee and I wanted to buckle. I wanted to tell him to touch me… there.

"*Please James,*" I gasped, almost moaning at the soft, wicked touch of his fingers nearing my inner thigh.

His jaw clenched, and I blinked at him with surprise when he pulled back, standing up and looking away from me. He even kept a distance from me, standing a few steps back.

"James I'm so—"

"Do you like them?"

"What?"

"The heels, Mia."

Oh, so now I was Mia?

Feeling dejected again, I looked away from him and at my feet. They were cute. Just like the dress, and I hated how good both of them made me look because I wanted to buy both of them. Only if I had brought my wallet with me.

"I asked you something."

I huffed, hearing the sternness in his voice. "Yes, I like them."

He narrowed his eyes at my face, but held back whatever he was going to say. He was pretending that whatever happened between us seconds ago didn't happen.

"Go change. We will be late for the dinner."

I rolled my eyes at him and shut myself in the changing room. Stripping out of the dress, I tried on the bikini. It flattered my small breasts and fit perfectly around my hips. The little red cherries on the light pink were a literal cherry on top.

"Mia. What's taking you so long?"

I bit my tongue from saying, *I'm rubbing one out. Wanna help?*

"I'm trying on the bikini. Do you want to see—"

"No. Be quick about it." His reply was sharp.

Well, then.

I patted down my hair when I got out of the changing room dressed in my uniform and holding the heels, dress, and bikini.

"I'll get them tomorrow when I have my—"

He took the items from my arms and took a step closer, looking down at me. "I don't like to repeat myself, Mia, so listen to me clearly. When I said I'll reward you and get you anything you want, I meant it. I don't care if you buy just these three things or the entire store. Understood?"

My mouth felt dry, and I nodded quickly, licking my lips.

"Say you understand, Princess."

"I-I understand."

His eyes softened. James smiled at me, leaning down and kissing my cheek before whispering, "Good girl."

I swallowed the lump in my throat when he pulled away, asking me if I wanted anything else. I shook my head before even thinking or looking at more items, because I couldn't spend one more minute alone in his presence without having the urge to kiss him. Or do something totally greedy and selfish like ask him to touch me between my legs.

It doesn't mean anything.

I stood beside him at the checkout and felt self-conscious just being on his side. I felt awkward yet a little turned on that James was holding the cart with the clothes and heels. I knew he didn't think about it, but it mattered to me a lot.

"I should bring my wallet," I grumbled when we were the next customers at checkout.

The employer smiled at us as she scanned our items.

James glanced at me and said in a firm voice, "I said I'd pay for it." He slid the shiny black card to her, making me and her double take on it. He was definitely rich, *rich*.

She gladly took the card and swiped it, smiling at me. "Yes, hon. Let your daddy pay for it."

My cheeks warmed. She thought he was my... daddy?

"She's n—"

"Yes, of course." I grinned at her, giving my daddy a side hug and feeling him stiffening underneath my touch. "I'll let my daddy pay for it."

Flickering my eyes at James, I found him forcing a smile at the employee as she packed our items in a paper bag and handed it to him. He took the bag before I could and wrapped his arm around me, dragging me away from the employee as I waved at her, giggling underneath my breath.

"Thank you for spoiling me, *Daddy*." I emphasized the last word, blinking at him.

His dark gaze drifted to me and I was surprised to find the similar expression on his face as before, when he found out I was wet. His hold tightened on my waist and I took a shuddering breath, feeling the hard ridges of his muscles through his shirt.

James leaned down and brushed his lips on my ear, making me shiver. "Don't call me that again unless you want to be punished for it, Princess."

"P-punished?"

"Of course. Spoiled little brats like you need to be punished by their daddies so they don't misbehave." He tilted his head, his expression serious. "Wouldn't you say so?"

9

IS IT HARD ENOUGH?

JAMES

I wanted her to shake her head and call me her daddy again.

It was fucked up, but I wanted to take her over my knee and spank her cute little ass until she begs me to touch her. Especially when she kept looking at me with her wide doe eyes like an innocent vixen. As if her white little panties weren't wet.

Fuck. Get a hold on yourself.

The trill of my phone alarm made me pull away from her. I ignored the way I missed her warmth and cherry scent and turned off the alarm. It was a reminder to reach Clyde's home for dinner.

Dinner with a naughty little vixen. And my friend who's her father.

Well, dinner was going to be hard. Literally.

"Let's go home."

Thankfully, Mia said nothing the whole ride home. Unfortunately, it made the tension between us increase and I had to force my hands on the steering wheel because she kept squirming in the seat. Her fingers curled tightly over her school skirt, and it was a good reminder for my self-control.

Not only she was my friend's daughter, I was also her teacher.

* * *

DINNER WAS BORING WITHOUT MIA. The tacos felt like chewing through rocks even though they were delicious because Clyde's cooking was one of the best I've ever had.

"She's locked up and doing her assignments," Clyde said when I took a small breather in the washroom.

I had to get away from Mia and her sweet cherry perfume. Had to wash my face with cold water and take a hard look in the mirror. She was fucking seventeen and my friend's daughter. My student, too.

It could never happen. Whatever we had between us. Even though she gets her little white panties soaked just by being near me, and I want to find out how she'd moan when I—

"Is it hard enough?"

I coughed and looked at Clyde's green eyes across the dining table. *I don't think he saw my hard on, did he?* That'd be fucking weird.

"What?"

He nodded at the tacos on my plate. "Shell. Is it hard enough? I used a different recipe for it this time."

I swallowed the lump in my throat and nodded. "It's perfect."

"They're delicious, Dad!"

I stiffened hearing that voice and took a huge bite of taco to stop myself from saying anything and shifted in my chair to hide the raging boner she had caused.

Mia must have taken a shower, because her dark locks

were damp. Her top was short with cute lace details and her shorts clung to her ass when she leaned over the kitchen counter to pile her plate with more tacos I couldn't help myself. I really couldn't as my eyes drifted to her long, toned legs. Her calves tensing when she stretched and her ass perked up.

I exhaled through my nose and licked my lips, remembering the soft touch of her skin when I had strapped her heels to her feet. How creamy her thighs were and the hot vision of her panties with a wet spot…

I wondered if she was wearing the same underwear and if it was soaked.

"I heard your first day was uneventful, Pumpkin," Clyde said to Mia as she walked over to the dining table and pulled out a chair.

"Day isn't over yet." Her eyes flickered to me. "Besides, I think the dean gave detention to Summer and Em is having boyfriend trouble. *Again*."

I took another bite, relishing in the delicious taste of tangy sauce and vegetables. "The dean seems a bit harsh, doesn't she?"

Mia shrugged. "She has never bothered me before, but I've heard from others that she is very strict."

"What about the boyfriend trouble? I didn't know she was dating," her dad asked. I ignored the pang in my heart seeing them. At the jealousy that boiled inside me. I wish I had a father like him who would have taken an interest in my life, or at least my school, to ask me about it during dinner.

"I told you about him, Dad. They were all here last week." She swallowed the food and said, licking her lips even though there was a bit of sauce smeared on the corner of her lips. "Emma's family is the trouble. They don't like him. Which is their problem. Frankly, Caleb is a great guy and treats her really well."

Her father narrowed his eyes at her. "Do you have a crush on someone?"

Red blush creeped up her neck to her cheeks and ears as she lied shaking her head. "No." Her eyes peered at me from her thick lashes before she glanced away, noticing my smirk. "I don't."

"That's good. I don't want to give your boyfriend a pep talk just yet. I'm too young for that."

She rolled her eyes. "Dad, you met Mom when you were in school."

Clyde chuckled and looked at me. "Tell her that times have changed. I don't trust guys in her school."

"Your father's right." I slid my eyes to her and smiled. "You shouldn't date a guy your age."

Her eyes gleamed, and she caught the undertone of my words. She took another bite so she wouldn't have to reply.

"What about you, James?" Clyde asked me. "Are you seeing anyone? I think you mentioned Julia last time."

"We are not dating. You know I don't date, Clyde. I've had my hands full with the company and now... *school*." I said the last word, looking directly at Mia, who was squirming in her seat.

The tips of her damp hair had made her top wet, and I was getting an eye full of her chest. I took a huge sip of beer and looked away.

Temptress. That's what she was. A fucking temptress.

We exchanged gifts during a rewatch of *The Walking Dead*. I felt extremely grateful to be a part of the family dinner for over a year because of how much joy it brought me seeing Clyde and Mia banter and share gifts. It felt like home.

Especially when they laughed over the funny gifts and gave me equally silly ones.

Mia had given me a mask of Ghostface, and Clyde gave me an invitation for a birthday party. My finger rubbed over the floral, intricate design of the card. An eighteenth birthday celebration for Mia in less than two weeks.

"Dad!" she whined, hiding her face in a quilt. "I told you I didn't want any party."

"I want you to celebrate it, Pumpkin. With your friends and old man. You'll be a lady soon."

She looked up and pouted at her father, then at me. "Then why did you give James an invitation?"

"Because he's family, right, James?"

All I could do was nod, seeing Mia frown. She stayed quiet and held the stuffed baby elephant I had gotten her because she liked stuffed toys, and I was more than willing to be useful for her collection. We both had run out of ideas to gift her dad, so we had bought him a ticket for an entire day at a spa so he could relax. She even paid half of it from her savings, even when I tried to reject it.

* * *

I CHECKED the time on my watch, and it was almost past midnight. We had watched three episodes of the series and Clyde was passed out on his recliner chair while Mia had already gone upstairs to sleep in early because it was a school night.

Pulling the quilt off of the couch, I tucked it over Clyde and turned off the television.

"Goodnight, old man," I whispered to him and picked up my cellphone, checking the kitchen island if I had to clean anything. But Mia and I had stocked the dishwasher together, and the counter was clean.

I went upstairs to say goodbye to Mia if she was awake when I heard it...

The smallest, softest whimper coming through her door.

"James..."

10

WILL YOU TEACH ME?

MIA

I touched my breasts through the thin tank top and sighed. It felt good. But it wasn't enough.

"James..." a small whimper elicited from my throat as I imagined his large hands caressing my skin. Holding my breasts, pinching and rolling my nipples.

My back arched, and I felt an intense rush of arousal, my clit throbbing for attention. I wanted more. So much more. I whimpered again, cupping myself through the shorts and bit my lip at the warm touch.

"Mia." A sharp knock made me freeze. I quickly sat up on the bed, straightening my clothes as if I was caught with my hands in a cookie jar. *But this was probably ten times worse than that.*

"Yes, come in." I leaned back on the headrest, pretending to read a book.

James opened the door and looked at me with a dark expression on his face. *Did he hear me? No. I don't think he did.*

"Clyde fell asleep on his recliner and... what are you reading?" He raised his brow, crossing his arms and showing off his delectable arms.

Fuck me.

"I'm reading romance." I met his stare and said, "It has friends to lovers trope, and it's really cute."

"I'm sure it is." A small smile curled at the corner of his lips as he glanced at the said book in my hands and said, "Princess, you're holding it upside down."

I glanced down and sure enough, I was holding it upside down. I was in a hurry when he had knocked and didn't notice the mistake.

Fuck me twice. I gingerly straightened it and cleared my throat, looking anywhere else but at him even though I felt his intense stare on my face, heating it up.

"What were you really doing, Mia?" he asked, his voice much closer than before and I swallowed the lump in my throat when I felt him invade my sanctuary.

"I... I was doing no—"

I gasped when he touched my face, cupping my jaw and making me look at him, meeting his piercing blue eyes. His touch was warm and electric. I wanted to lean in and kiss him. His thumb brushed over my cheekbone as he whispered,

"Don't lie."

It was a warning. Which I didn't listen to because lying and teasing him was more fun. I wanted to unravel him. See what was beneath the facade of a hot billionaire-slash-teacher. See what kind of person he was underneath his crisp shirts and slacks.

"Or what, Daddy?"

I felt immense pleasure when his eyes dilated hearing my words, shock and surprise flickering through his face. But he didn't pull away. No, he tightened his hold on my jaw and narrowed his eyes at me, his hot breath fanning over my cheeks.

"I warned you about calling me that again, you naughty little Princess."

I squirmed, hearing the growl in his voice and the promise of danger with pleasure lacing it. His eyes flickered to my legs, and I gasped again when he parted them, holding my thigh.

"Did you touch yourself thinking about me?" he cooed, his hand caressing my thigh while the other brushed my hair over my shoulder, brushing his fingers lightly over my neck and shoulder, making me shiver at his feather-light touches. "Did you touch your sweet little cunt thinking about Daddy?"

My cheeks burned and eyes glazed. *Was it a dream? Or was James really, really touching me? Calling me a naughty little Princess?* Not only that, but I was immensely enjoying it.

"Tell me, Princess." He cocked his head. "Or do you call me Mister James when you cum, *hm?* Which one is it?"

"I-I..." I shook my head, too embarrassed to answer him.

"I wasn't asking you." James grabbed my hair, gently tugging it and making my clit ache more when he leaned closer and said, "That was an order. Tell me."

"I..." Tears sprang up in my eyes when I said the frustrating truth, "I can't cum."

James didn't scoff or roll his eyes at me like I thought he would. Instead, he softened his hold on my hair and raked his hand through it. It felt nice to know that he couldn't stop touching me.

"You can't cum or couldn't cum, Princess?" he asked, pulling away, and I had to bite down on my lower lip to stop myself from whimpering at the loss of his warm touch. I didn't want him to stop touching me. *Ever.*

I glanced at my fidgeting fingers and answered, "I can't."

"That's nonsense."

"It's not!" I glared at him, my throat burned, and I wanted

to cry because it was both embarrassing and shameful. I didn't even know how to pleasure myself or kiss or go on dates, while my friends and girls my age were hooking up left and right. I felt left out. I didn't want to be a wallflower when it came to intimacy.

"Anyone can orgasm, Mia. You just don't know how to touch yourself the right way."

I swallowed the lump in my throat and peered at his angular face through my lashes, "Will you teach me?"

He blinked at me. "What?"

Shifting on the bed, I knelt on the mattress and crawled towards him where he was standing on the edge of the bed. I stayed on my knees and looked up at him. "Teach me." I took a shaky breath and repeated, "Teach me how to touch myself, James."

He was quiet for a moment before he took a lock of my hair and rubbed it between his fingers. "Is that how you want to address your teacher, your dad's best friend? Or was it Daddy?"

My entire body flushed but it was too late. We both had crossed that line.

"What do you want me to call you?"

"I think we both know the answer to that."

"D-daddy?"

He smiled, his large hand caressing my cheek. "Yes, Princess?"

I leaned into his touch and said, "Will you teach me how to cum?"

James bent down to look me straight in the eye and said, "What will I get in return?"

I squirmed feeling the pressure between my legs increase. It was like all the times I would wake up from wet dreams. It was an aching need to hold his hand and lead it between my thighs so he could touch me exactly where I wanted him the most.

His eyes noted my movements and he clucked his tongue in a stern matter. My lips parted when he wrapped his hand around my throat, just holding it, and my ache increased tenfold.

"I asked you a question, Princess. Stay still and answer."

"Or what?"

His hold tightened on my neck and I gasped, wrapping my hand around his forearm. "That's twice you forgot to address me correctly. I won't be gentle next time."

He was being gentle?!

His hold softened, but he kept his grip on my neck and oddly enough, it felt nice. I felt owned, his. His... *something*.

"Or what, Daddy?" I asked, licking my lips and clenching my legs.

"Or I won't teach you how to cum, you naughty brat," James said with a small smile as if he was enjoying this. His words didn't match the emotions flickering through his face, and it made me want to tease him more. Ruffle his feathers.

"Please, Daddy?" I even pouted and batted my lashes, hoping he would just hold my face and kiss me.

His eyes flickered to my mouth. "Tell me what I get in return."

"Anything you want, Daddy."

James tilted his head as his hand pulled away to stroke my neck. The pads of his fingers brushed over my hammering pulse when his dark eyes raked over the length of my body as if he was assessing me.

"Anything I want, *hm?*"

I nodded, leaning into his soft caresses. I didn't know we had shifted so close to each other. He smelled of pine and fresh woods and his breath caressed my bare skin. I wanted to bask in his scent and wanted it all over me. Over my bed.

"*Anything.*"

"Even fucking you?" he asked, my eyes widening when he whispered in my ear, "Strip you out of the clothes I buy you and take you in every way possible. Make your little cunt cream around my cock while fucking you like my princess slut."

He pulled away, noticing my heaving chest and how hard I was clenching my thighs together to get some sort of friction on my clit.

"Will you let me fuck you, Mia? If I make you cum like the good girl you are, hm?"

11

YES, DADDY

JAMES

"Will you let me fuck you, Mia? If I make you cum like the good girl you are, hm?"

Say no. Please. For the sake of my sanity, pull away, slap me, curse me, do anything but agree.

"Y-yes," Mia whispered, her hazel-green eyes dilated and hazy as she answered, "Yes, Daddy."

Fuck, fuck, fuck.

This wasn't supposed to happen. Any of it.

I was supposed to bid her goodnight, drive back to a penthouse that's too big for me, fuck my fist until I spilled all over my stomach and sleep alone on a cold bed then wake up next morning with guilty conscience while dressing up for school.

But I'm a sinner through and through. *Like father, like son.*

I brushed my thumb over her plump bottom lip and demanded, "Say it again, Princess."

"Yes, Daddy."

"No," I tsked. "Tell me what filthy things I'll do to you if I make you cum."

"I…" She took a shuddering breath and squirmed. *Fuck me.* Her nipples were hard and slicing through the thin top she was wearing, and I'd sever my own fucking hand to have a taste of those perfect tits. Wrap my mouth around her hard little nipples and suck. I got back to Earth when she whispered, "You'll fuck me, Daddy. However you want. I'll do anything. Please."

Oh how beautifully she begged. I wanted to taint her more. I craved it like a druggie craved cocaine. She was my drug and I craved her more than anything.

"You can beg better than that, can't you, Princess?" I crooned, stroking her cheek as if I was praising and humiliating her at the same time.

But she didn't wince or pull away like I had imagined her to. Most women in her place would have. Unfortunately, I had been on the receiving end of disgusting looks and even a couple of slaps, even though I had explicitly explained about my kinks in the bedroom.

But not Mia.

No, she fucking leaned into my hand and nodded, "Yes, please fuck me, Daddy. I'll do anything you want in return."

I wasn't expecting her to accept all my filthy wishes—wishes that she didn't even know about yet agreed to. *Oh how I ached to taint her.*

"What a dirty thing to say to your Daddy, you naughty brat," I said and pulled some space between us. It hurt not to touch her, but I needed to pull back from her cherry scent and her addictive soft skin.

"W-what happened?" Her eyes were half-lidded and if I asked to fuck her then and there, I was sure she would just nod prettily and spread her soft thighs welcoming me.

I was a sadistic sinner, but even I had my own limits.

"I promise to make you cum, Princess." I kissed her forehead, and pulled back, "But not today."

"No! That's not fair." She was angry and her eyes gleamed with frustrated tears.

Poor Princess.

"Behave and I'll reward you soon," I promised.

"How soon, Daddy?"

I narrowed my eyes at her. "Go to bed, Mia. It's a school night."

"Whatever. Go away." She scoffed and looked away from me.

Oh, she was definitely a brat.

I smirked. I would have a fun time punishing her. "That's the third time you forgot to address me, Princess. I'll remind you of that when I punish you." Her eyes widened when she noticed how serious I was about her punishment. "Goodnight, Princess."

Before I closed the door to her room behind me, I heard her whisper, "Goodnight, Daddy."

I took a deep breath and glanced down at the bulge pressing against my zipper. *Fucking my fist, it is.*

* * *

"And how would you turn this paper into 3D?" I asked, holding the hard paper with a thick gsm.

Some students were leaning on the desk with a frown on their faces and the others were going through their notes as if an answer would appear to them magically.

"By folding it?" Mia asked, raising her hand.

"Almost correct answer." I went back to my desk and taught them how to hold a cutter. A forty-five-degree angle, where to grip it and how to move it on the paper instead of pressing it.

I made a few cuts using a stainless-steel ruler for folding

the paper and using the cutter. Once I was happy with my design, I passed it to my students.

"That's how you turned a two-dimensional paper into three-dimensional." As each one of them held it up to their face and moved it around, I explained to them about the open and closed spaces. Talking about negatives and positives.

"Now I can create whatever I want to with this space. For example, a bus stop with this roof acting as a shelter. I can put benches here and a few commercials here." I pointed out each space and I was glad to see awed faces from the students. I had a similar expression on my face when my professor in college started teaching about space and how anyone could have fun with it and make anything out of it. It was both creative and a mentally stimulating exercise.

"Are you guys excited to try it?" I asked with a raised brow and a resonating 'yes' followed through the classroom. I grinned and helped them with the materials.

"You can do whatever you want for your first three tries, but you'll have to explain to the entire classroom what you have built."

Emma raised her hand and I asked her to continue. "Can we use anything we want? Colors, glitters?"

Giggles spiraled through the other girls and I shrugged, "Use whatever you want, Emma. Even color papers are a great option, but you have to define the space. It can be a maze, a bridge, underground tunnel, game, anything. Let your mind fly."

I didn't have to tell them to start folding with rulers and creating the spaces their head desired because all of them were already scrambling for their papers.

The next hour passed by in a blur of helping a few students on how to hold the cutter, use the ruler for folding and even letting them draw, sketch and paint on the papers before they could make a three-dimensional model. It was a chaos, but it was a creative chaos. The best kind.

"Do you need help with those, Mister James?" I looked up from the desk and smiled at the student when she pointed out the extra materials.

"No, thank you. We will need this for next lessons."

"Oh." She twirled her dark lock of hair, looking away and asked, "Is there anything else I can help you with? Like do you need a personal assistant?"

I frowned, ready to decline her when Emma and Mia walked up to my desk. "Seriously, Claire? He is an art teacher." I tried my best not to frown more when Emma kept her hand on her hip and gave a scathing look to her classmate. "Why would he need a personal assistant?"

"I was just asking. Not everyone has butlers and maids like you. I wanted to help Mister James."

Emma rolled her eyes and muttered something underneath her breath that made Mia choke and her cheeks redden. She looked cute and I wanted to pull her on my lap and ask if she enjoyed the lesson. I wanted to ask her about her models and pick apart her brain.

Shaking off those thoughts, I stood up, towering over them and answered, "Thank you, Claire, for asking me, but I don't need a personal assistant at the moment. I already have one that handles all my tasks so, if you'll excuse me. Have a good day."

I didn't need to elaborate that my personal assistant also handled my entire constructing business while I was teaching and didn't have extra hours in the day to look after my design class.

I unlocked my phone and checked the notifications. I had it in a silent mode for the class. Scowling, I called Clyde's number. He had called me over three times and it was very unusual. Even if his house was burning, he'd just send a text message with a few emojis because he thought calling people would disturb their 'flow,' whatever fuck that meant.

An uneasy feeling grew in my belly as I stood in the corner of the hallway, hearing the phone ring.

"Pick up, dammit."

"James…"

I didn't need to know who the person was when they touched my arm. I pinned my eyes on her green orbs that were gleaming with tears, and I knew something had happened.

"It's D-Dad."

12
PINKY PROMISE

MIA

I didn't know what to think. How to think. All my motor functions had come to a halt as soon as I had heard a very patient nurse through the phone. Thankfully, Emma and Summer had cornered me seeing my pale face and kept the phone on speaker, hearing the second worst news I've ever heard in seventeen years of my life.

First one was when my dad brought me into that god-awful hospital room and told me what had happened to Mom.

"Mia."

I couldn't breathe. My arms were shaking, and I wanted to empty my breakfast—*oh God, my dad...* he had made eggs, and we had joked about something this morning, and we were laughing and he—

"*Mia.*" My vision was getting blurry as I focused on the sharp, intense gaze. His warm hands on my shoulder. "I'm here. Clyde is okay."

"H-He..." I shook my head, tears streaming down my face. I didn't want to think. I wanted to throw myself in cold water and never breathe just so I could stop the ache in my heart.

I didn't want to feel this emotion again. Not so soon. Never again. I had tried not to feel it for years, and I won't be able to deal with it now.

"Let's go. I'm taking you there." He didn't wait for my reply. Wrapping his hand around mine, he dragged me out of the busy hallway to the parking lot. I was scrambling to meet his pace, but he didn't rush me, he met my pace, tightening his hold on my hand and opening the car door for me.

"James, he—"

He knelt in front of me when I was seated on the passenger seat. He cupped my cheeks and wiped the tears with his thumbs, slowly stroking my hair. His blue eyes burned with sincerity as he whispered, "He is Clyde. He'll be okay. If anything happens… I'm here, Mia. I'm not going anywhere. I'll stay with you."

I nodded shakily, clutching his wrist, and closed my eyes to relish the warm feeling when he kissed my forehead. It was okay. James said it was okay, so it must be. He promised me he'll stay. *James keeps his promises, doesn't he?*

I didn't know when and how he strapped a seatbelt over me or what I said or didn't on the way. I was too busy overthinking the worst-case scenarios and wondering if it was an early prank for my birthday.

But I know James held my hand the entire ride. His warm, long fingers entwined with my small ones and how each knuckle fit perfectly with mine. The pad of his thumb made soft strokes on my skin, and it eased the bubbling nervousness that was ready to erupt out of me in heaving sobs.

I had already lost my mom. I didn't want to lose—

No. I won't. Nothing was going to happen to him.

He's just pranking all of us.

"Mia, we're here." His voice was soft when he parked the car and unbuckled my seat belt. I clutched his hand the entire time. Clenching his arm underneath my fingers when the scent of medicine and detergent hit my nose. It wasn't loud and people talked in hushed voices, doctors giving sad or happy news to a family, nurses helping patients and... it was just too much.

The glaring white lights looked sickly, and I wanted to crawl out of my skin. A strong arm wrapped around my waist and pulled me close to the warmth of his chest. I sighed and listened to his heartbeat to calm myself as we reached the floor of his room.

James guided me towards the room where my dad was and I let go of him only to see the shutters over the glass panel of the room.

"You must be Clyde's daughter." I turned towards the woman in a white coat with a stethoscope around the collar. "Hello, dear, I'm Doctor Ekta."

"When can I see him? Is he okay?"

"You can see him when he wakes up from a surgery. He experienced a subarachnoid hemorrhage, and he'll need to undergo a surgery for a coil placement."

I didn't care what happened to him. I wanted him with me. Ruffle my hair and call me his Pumpkin. Nothing else mattered.

I sat down on the metal chair outside his room and clutched my phone tightly in my hand. Summer and Emma had told me to keep them updated, but I didn't know what to say. *Hey, Summer, Em, my dad had aneurysm and will undergo surgery soon. Not sure if he'll be alive or not by the end, though. At least the doctor is pretty sweet. XOXO.*

Before I could hide my face and sob, a small bottle of chocolate milkshake appeared in front of me. My eyes drifted to the person holding the bottle.

"I don't want it."

"I wasn't asking, Princess." He raised his brow, blue eyes staring down at me. "Drink it."

My stomach grumbled at the sight, and I took the milkshake, keeping it aside. James sighed and sat down beside me, his thigh pressing against mine.

We sat in silence for a few minutes. My dad had complained about a headache in the morning and he collapsed at his office. Thankfully, one of his colleagues noticed and called an ambulance.

"Tell me good news," I said, glaring at the white paint of the wall across from me. I hated everything about hospitals.

"Clyde has thirty percent chance of survival rate."

I swallowed the lump in my throat and chuckled. "Of course, that's the good news."

"Well, his survival rate would be ten percent if he didn't arrive at the hospital in time." He took a deep breath and turned towards me. "He'll have surgery soon, and when he wakes up, he will remember you and scold you for missing half a day at school."

I pursed my lips as my throat burned. I wanted to cry. "You're the one who dragged me here. He'll scold you, too."

James gave me a soft smile and kissed my cheek. "He'll be okay, Princess. I'll make sure of it."

My heart felt heavy hearing his words.

"Promise?"

He raised his hand and said, "Pinky promise."

I entwined my pinky finger with his and pressed our thumbs together, sealing the promise. By the look in his eyes, I knew he would do anything to keep his word.

I trusted him.

I knew my dad would be alright. He'd survive.

* * *

"ARE you sure you don't want steamed rice with the curry—"

I made a face behind his back. "No, thank you. I'll make some ramen."

James froze and turned around. He was wearing a 'Call me DADDY' apron, which oddly enough, suited him.

It was illegal how he could wear anything and make it look hot.

"Can you even boil water without burning down the house?" he asked, keeping his hand on his hip.

"Of course I can!" My cheeks turned red, and I defended myself. "Last week, I boiled the water and cooked the noodles."

He nodded, plating food in a Tupperware. "Sure you did. The noodles were salty and half uncooked, so you ended up ordering a takeout. *Again*."

I sulked on my stool, fiddling with the loops of tie that I was still learning from YouTube. I missed my dad. I wished he would tie my tie and call me his Pumpkin.

It had been over a week since my dad had surgery and a metal clip was placed inside his head. I know, it was scary cool. Summer joked about how he won't be able to walk through metal detectors, and Emma corrected her, saying it was a titanium chip.

He could walk through metal detectors as soon as he could walk again. The doctor had mentioned atrophy, but it had hurt to see him in a hospital bed all day or use a wheelchair. He had to spend a few more days in the hospital while he underwent therapy to regain his ability to walk.

"You're looping it wrong—*here*, let me teach you how to do this..." James walked towards me and stood too close. His long fingers expertly moving through the loops. I noticed the stubble on his sharp jaw and wanted to ask if he was doing okay.

He was close to my father, after all. It must have hurt him, too. Not to mention having to spend time in the house, cooped up with me and my annoying self for the past week.

Did I annoy him? Did I ask for too much sweets and junk food? I wanted to ask him, but I trusted James to be honest about his feelings.

On the good side, I had been laser focused on my studies and eating delicious healthy meals of James' cooking. I had joked that if he hadn't become an architect, he could definitely go try his hand at being a chef, and he revealed to me that his mother was a chef.

My dad had mentioned that James was an orphan, but we never talked about his parents. It must be too painful for him.

Grief. Loss. Death. All these emotions took a lot of courage to talk about, and I'd wait until James felt comfortable enough to talk to me about them.

"Mia." There was a small smile on his lips when I pulled out of my head. "Did you learn anything, or were you too busy drooling at me?"

"I was not drooling at you…" *Wait, was I? Do I have drool on my chin?* Ohmygod. Kill me. "I… I don't think I have motor skills to tie any knot," I said, frowning at the perfect tie James did. "Where did you learn to tie a tie?"

His eyes darkened as he fixed my collars and smoothened my shirt. My heartbeat fluttered at his little touch. It was such a domesticated action that I wanted him to pull me closer and—

No. Bad thoughts.

"I learned it from a lot of things."

"Such as?"

His blue gaze pinned on me. "Trust me, Princess. You don't want to know."

"No, I want to know. I want to learn how to tie…" My words died in my throat when he leaned closer.

"I know how to tie up pretty little princesses like you when they don't behave and eat their veggies." My jaw dropped when he tugged at my tie and pulled away. He slid the Tupperware to me and crossed his arms, his face stern. "I want to see that empty after lunch."

"Or what?" I asked angrily, shoving my lunch in my bag and glaring at him. "You're going to tie me up and punish me, Daddy?"

He narrowed his eyes, and I had to hold my breath when he whispered in a low, husky voice, "I just might, Princess."

13

BRING A SWIMSUIT

JAMES

"Why didn't you tell me it was this bad?" I asked, trying to rein in the anger and guilt that I felt. "You could've told me."

Clyde didn't look at me. "I didn't tell anyone because no one was supposed to know."

"Clyde," I said, sitting down on the chair and facing him. "I can help—"

"No," he answered, finally meeting my eyes. "No, James. You've done enough for my family and I can't—I won't accept it now. I'll go back to work as soon as I get out of this damn hospital and it'll be alright."

I closed my eyes and leaned back in the chair. It was a mess.

"I take it Mia doesn't know that her tuition fees for the next semester aren't paid yet and her father is paying off his debt, so you can't pay for your own medications." I glanced around the room and said dryly, "Or the hospital bill."

Clyde sighed and rubbed his hand over his face. He looked tired and exhausted. At least he was alive. I should be thankful for that.

I swallowed the lump in my throat. "Promise me one thing, Clyde."

"What's that?"

"Walk out of this hospital and have one of our traditional dinners at your house. Do that and you don't have to worry about anything." My throat burned but fuck it, he was the only person who had ever looked at me and saw my worth when even I couldn't. He was the father I had never had. "I give you my word."

Clyde gave me a sad smile and reached out to ruffle my hair. "It'll be alright, son."

"Dad?"

We both froze and turned towards the door where Mia stood in her school uniform wearing a shocked expression on her face.

"Hey, Pumpkin."

She blinked and looked at both of us. "So no take outs for a while, huh?"

After a few minutes of awkward silence, Mia was seated in the chair closest to Clyde's bed and her friends Emma and Caleb shuffled at the edge of the bed. I wasn't surprised to hear that Emma drove Mia to the hospital, but I didn't know they would come up to meet him.

Seeing the way Clyde hugged Emma and shook Caleb's hand, they were all close.

"Where's Summer?" Clyde asked after Mia talked about school and I tried my best to glare at the book I was holding. They both were avoiding the elephant in the room and avoiding talking about it.

"She got detention. Again. She told us to go ahead and oh —Mister Clyde, you better start walking because I'm hosting Mia's birthday party this weekend," Emma said, offering him a lilac pink envelope which smelled fruity. I wondered if there was glitter too.

"I'm not having a birthday party anymore," Mia said, frowning at her friends.

"Come on, Clyde will join us for a few beers, won't he, James?" Caleb asked, winking at me, and I wanted to hurl the book at him for ever thinking I was on a first-name basis with him.

"No, he won't," Mia said firmly. "I'm maintaining his diet and I don't want to have—"

"Pumpkin. You'll turn eighteen only once in a lifetime." He patted her hair and I once again looked away, clenching the book in my hand. "Go spend some time with your friends."

No one wanted to argue to a forty-year-old father who just had a surgery for an aneurysm, so we left the room. Before I could grab a can of dark black coffee and hot chocolate, Emma stopped me, handing me the similar pink envelope with my name written in cursive with a glitter pen. Oddly enough, it was adorable. But I won't ever tell her that.

"This is for you." Somehow, she managed to sniff down at me with her small frame. She crossed her arms. "Only because Mia likes you and my mom wanted me to invite you."

Her mom? Must be none other than the icy Dorothy Moore. Renowned retired actress who moved from the city of fame and glamour, Los Angeles, to a small town with creeks, like Coral Springs, to settle with her family. Which included just her and her daughter, Emma.

Ah. It was going to be an interesting party.

"Bring a swimsuit," she said, and turned around.

"See you at school, teach." Caleb gave me a two-finger salute and wrapped his arm around Emma's shoulder as they walked out of my sight.

I sighed and pocketed the envelope. I might visit the infamous Moore house if I was interested. I was about to walk into Clyde's hospital room when I heard the high-pitched voice of a certain someone.

"But Dad, I saved up for it myself and we can use it to pay the bills—"

"I'd rather work myself to the grave paying off another debt than take your hard-earned money, Pumpkin."

My jaw clenched at the thought of Mia thinking about paying off her father's medical bills. As if I'd ever let her.

"I sold cupcakes, Dad. I don't care. I... I know it won't be enough, but don't worry, I'll do something."

"Mia." I heard Clyde whisper, calling his daughter by her first name. "I don't want you to worry about money, okay? I survived and after a few days, I'll be out of here. I'll make you eggs and tie your tie. Just take care of yourself and focus on school. Let your old man worry about you."

"Dad." Her voice broke and my hand clenched on the door handle before I took a step back and walked away.

Images of turned over car and blood flashed in my head as I thought about how young and reckless I was when that accident had happened. Even then, Clyde was the only person who looked at me and told me it wasn't my fault. I had wanted to die, and he saved me.

Now, I was going to repay all his debts tenfold. After all, he was the only person who ever had my back.

* * *

"Yeah—you like that, you little slut."

I stopped mid shave and frowned at my reflection in the mirror. *What the fuck was happening?*

It had been a week since I moved in to Clyde's home to take care of Mia and make sure she was coping well. During the entire time I was in the house, I either stumbled into Mia half-naked with a face mask on and dancing to dramatic songs of Taylor Swift, having a pretend breakup with one of her stuffed toys (it's usually a kangaroo because the cartoon eyes look really sad), or she's dead-asleep whenever she could find a comfortable place.

She's like a cat. Or a kitten. Falling asleep on the kitchen stool, in an empty bathtub with clothes on (yes, I almost left her there seeing her cocooned so comfortably inside a bathtub), on the floor with her face planted on the rug.

I could go on and on about how odd she lived (maybe it's because she's a Gen Z),but hearing those words in a growly moaning voice of a man made me wonder about all the choices I had made before to end up at this moment, naked with a towel wrapped around my waist, my jaw covered in shaving foam.

"You want me to suck your little tiddies, babydoll? Yeah, mmm."

Visibly shuddering and cringing at the porn-y dialogue, I made my way out of the washroom after washing off the shaving foam. The guest room I'd been staying in was scattered with a few books, my laptop, and my clothes hanging in the closet.

My feet padded against the wooden floor, getting close towards Mia's room. I knocked, shaking my head at the guy who was full on fake moaning in the mic.

After losing my patience, I opened the door and found the little feline-like culprit on the bed.

14

NO, THANK YOU, DADDY

MIA

"You like that, don't you, babydoll? I bet your lil' cunny is soaked."

I whimpered and closed my eyes to try moaning sultry like the voice actor was doing over the speakers. But I found it awkward and a bit cringe-y that he was faking most of it. *He was, right? Or was it real?* I couldn't tell. I was too busy trying to find the right—

"Mia."

I squeaked and turned to look at the face of the man who was currently stripping me out of my night clothes in my head. *Oh God. Oh, my God. Why does everyone find the perfect time to disturb me every time I try to masturbate?*

I rolled over in my panic—fueled by embarrassment and a guilty conscious—and fell over the other side of the bed, almost hitting my head on the nightstand.

"Are you alright?" He came forward, but I was still in my panic fueled—*oh, you get the point.* I scrambled away from him, standing up too quickly and tripping with my foot on the blanket that was wrapped around my ankles.

I squeezed my eyes shut, ready to fall face-flat on the

floor, and insert a tampon in my nose when it bleeds for the next hour.

But, fortunately, that never happened.

Instead, I fell on a solid wall that was made of warm muscles. I opened one eye and ogled at my fingers that were touching the strong slabs of abs.

Oh yum.

A very male sound elicited near my ear that made goosebumps skitter all over my body.

"That's not very nice of you."

"Nice?" I glanced at his face and almost swallowed my tongue at the look in his eyes.

They were blazing with lust and he looked like he wanted to devour me—eat me alive. And oddly enough, I'd have let him, spreading my legs—

I shifted in his arms, loving the way they wrapped around me in a tight embrace. His hair was a little damp and so dark that I wanted to run my hands through it and press my nose against it. I know, it's me, Mia, the little hair creep. But I swear, I've never smelled anything so male, pine and *him* before.

"Mia," he groaned, pulling me closer and glaring down at me accusingly, as if I had done something—

"Stop fucking moving." He voiced out. "You're making this difficult."

"I-I'm not doing anything—*ohmy...* is that?" I tried to peer down, but my lovely, lucky girls were squished against his chiseled broad chest. "Is that... *you*?"

A groan.

"You're hard."

He glared. "Glad you noticed." Clenching his jaw, he added, "Hand me my towel."

"I don't have your towel."

"*Yes*—" he took a deep breath, closing his eyes and then

opening them. His blue eyes seemed way darker than before. *Was he on edge? Because of me?* I wanted to grin. "It's by your feet."

I relaxed in his arms and smiled up at him, tapping his nose with my finger, booping it. "I'm sure you can retrieve it by yourself, Daddy."

He raised his brow and held my jaw, narrowing his eyes at me. "I'm not playing with you and your bratty ass right now, Princess. Either turn around and close your eyes or hand me the towel like a good little girl."

Oh, fuck, now I want to play with him.

"*Hmmm.*" I batted my lashes at him and said in an innocent voice. "No, thank you, Daddy."

His fingers tightened on my skin and my breathing increased. I shivered at the sensation of feeling him twitch down there… *Oh god, he was big.* No, he was *BIG*. Yes, all caps were needed with italics. *Was that even possible? How would he even fit?* I squirmed, feeling my panties dampen at the mere thought of him holding me down and calling me sweet words while he thrusted inside me inch by glorious inch.

"*Fuck,*" he whispered in his deep, throaty voice. "You're thinking about it right now, aren't you, you dirty little girl?"

I shook my head but—

"Fuck, yeah. Suck me again you whor—"

My cheeks burned, and I quickly pulled away from James, turning around without even glancing down at him (mentally patting my back for the self-restraint) and switched off Alexa. I didn't say anything for a while because I was too busy hearing how he wrapped the towel around himself.

"Is that one of your night routine?"

"What is?"

He walked over to my desk and tilted his head at the screen of my phone. "Don't play dumb, Mia. You were listening to this for a release, weren't you?"

I bit my lip and crossed my arms, staring at his sexy back. How the muscles clenched and moved with him... and his ass. *Fuck me*. There was something hot about his ass.

"What if I was?" I asked, raising my chin. "You promised me an orgasm and left me."

James chuckled darkly and prowled towards me. Despite me being fully clothed in top and shorts, I felt more naked than him in a towel. He seemed to consume every part of space whenever we were alone, and he looked bigger, meaner, and scarier than before.

It turned me on.

I must have hit my head harder than I thought.

"I never promised you one orgasm, Princess," he said, trailing his finger over my cheek. "Were you close?"

"Close?"

"Close to cumming."

I looked away from his piercing eyes and shook my head. "I don't—I don't know."

He tsked. "Bratty little princess doesn't even know if she was close to an orgasm." He raised his palm and said, "Give me your hand."

Frowning, I offered him my palm. "What are you doin—mmfh*oh*."

I cupped my mouth when he took my hand and cupped my pussy with it over the shorts. Even though there were two fabrics of clothing, I felt sensitive and extremely turned on looking into James' eyes when he gazed at me like I was an open banquet just for him.

"You're wet and I haven't even touched you, Princess," he chuckled crudely, and despite feeling ashamed, I was hornier than ever.

"T-touch me, please, Daddy."

"*Hmm*, let me think about it." He tilted his head. "How about no, thank you, Princess?"

Fuck. Him.

James must have seen the anger on my face because he squeezed my pussy through my hand, making me whimper. He leaned closer to my face, his warm, minty breath brushing over my lips. "This is why good princesses should behave when their daddies tell them to do something."

He pulled away and moved my fingers like they were his over my clit. My knees buckled, struggling to stay steady on my feet.

"I was going to be nice and let you cum, but…"

"*But?*" I was going to cry if he left me again.

"But someone was being bratty. I'll have to punish them, won't I, Princess?" he cooed, slowly stroking my clit, watching me underneath his lashes as I moved my hips over both of our hands.

He was being cruel again. I hated it. But I loved it too. God, I was a mess.

"P-please Daddy?" My fingers clenched on his forearm, trying to increase the pace of my other fingers, but he wouldn't let me. *So cruel.*

"I fucking love it when you beg, Mia," he whispered, his pupils dilated. "And you'll beg me again to let you cum, but until then, you'll have to make do with your fingers." I whimpered when he pulled away.

"Rub your lil' cunny like that and you might cum, baby-doll." He winked at me and walked out of my room.

I glared at his stupid head, stupidly sexy back and that stupid hot ass as I cursed and slammed the door close.

He wanted to tease me then, fine. I'll tease him right back. *I was Mia fucking Miller and this time, he'll be the one begging me to touch him.*

* * *

"OH, YES, IT'S SO GOOD!" I moaned, licking the maple syrup from my index finger, staring at his face across the table and moaning again.

He sighed and looked down at the book he was reading while eating his breakfast. He looked up again in shock when I moaned loudly, taking the finger out of my mouth with a smacking *pop* that made his cheeks flushed.

"Okay, you can stop moaning now."

"No!" I drawled out the word 'o' and batted my lashes. "It's necessary to moan if I want to orgasm."

"Orgasm? Right now?" he deadpanned, staring at the plate of pancakes in front of me.

I leaned on the table and said in a hushed voice as if I was sharing a secret, "I read in Cosmopolitan that if I moan or make sexy sounds, I'll orgasm soon enough."

"Of course, you read that in Cosmopolitan." He closed his book and leaned on the table, his face inches away from me. *God, why does he always have to smell so fucking good?*

"Are you?"

"Am I what?"

"Are you going to orgasm soon enough?"

I frowned, and he smiled at me, showing off his perfect white teeth. "You aren't, *hm*? That's sad."

I shot daggers at his neck when he stood up from the stool. "It's not sad. I just need to try something different. Maybe I won't even need you for it, ha!"

He chuckled and ruffled my hair. "Whatever you say, Princess." I batted his hand away. "Behave today and if you're good, I'll take you out this evening."

My ears perked up. "Where?"

Was it a date? Maybe an early birthday present? Both?

"It's a surprise which I'm sure you'll love."

"What is it?"

"A sex toy."

I snickered and dug into my plate. Yeah, right. As if James was ballsy enough to take me to a freaking sex shop and get me a sex toy.

Yeah, right.

Wait... he wouldn't, right?

Right?

15
SEE ME AFTER CLASS

MIA

The thing started vibrating in my hand and I almost dropped it.

"You guys are insane," I breathed out, already pressing my thighs together as I stared at the egg thingy and between my two best friends, who were smirking at me.

I shook my head and turned it off. "I don't want it." Even though it looked... *handy*.

Summer grinned, "Too bad it's your birthday gift."

"It's *not* my birthday."

Emma rolled her baby blue eyes and continued applying a pink gloss over her lips, staring at her reflection in the mirror. "It's your early birthday gift, babe. We both ordered it a month ago to get it imported here from London, so you better use it and rate the O."

My cheeks burned, and I looked around the washroom again, just to make sure we were alone. It was lunch break and thankfully, the unisex washroom on the third floor of our building was empty. My friends had decided it was a great idea to surprise me with a little vibrator.

Spoiler Alert: It was not so little.

"Rate the O?" I repeated.

Summer fluffed her curls. "Yes, but I think it'd be more than one O. Oh, girl, you're going to see heaven."

I glanced down at the lilac pink vibrator that was egg-shaped, but it seemed somehow bigger with its bulbous part, making me feel... *strange*. It was odd, and I wasn't sure if I liked the strange feeling or not.

"You mean... I'll get multiple orgasms from this tiny thing?" I asked, dangling it between all three of us. It was made of body-safe silicone and had a little loop of string at the end. *It's even rechargeable*, Emma had said excitedly when I opened the gift box that they handed me.

"Caleb is extremely jealous that I have a few toys like these," Em said, flipping her blonde curls over her shoulder.

"He doesn't mind?"

"Why would he? TMI, but he sometimes likes to use them on me." Her cheeks flushed and my mind wandered to James and his dark eyes. His filthy words crooning in my ears while the electric buzz of the vibe is pressed against me and he makes me—

Oh.

"I don't think this is a good idea."

"Are you sure?" Summer asked, frowning at me. "You don't have to use it right away if you don't want to, but keep it with you."

"Mhm, also it has this remote if you are into that and all." Emma pointed at the tiny black remote in the box and continued as if my eyes weren't wide as saucers, "I wooed Summer to come shopping with me—"

"*Bribed*," Summer added, "She bribed me with a bookstore gift card."

"You should come with us. We can shop clothes for your birthday and spend some time together!"

I had not told them about how I was low on cash and James had already bought me everything I needed for the birthday. Because if I did, they would try to gift me something more expensive or write me a check and start calling James my sugar daddy. Which he wasn't.

"Sorry guys, I don't think I'll be able to come with you."

Emma frowned. "How about a sleepover?"

"Sure, sleepover sounds great!"

"I can come with you and we can go to Em's house together," Summer added, looking up from her phone, already adding it to her reminders.

I closed the lid of the gift box and said, "It's alright. I can get a cab."

Emma leaned closer and smiled with a mischievous glint in her eyes. "Or ask James to drop you."

"James, *huh?*" Summer wriggled her eyebrows at me.

"Hush, you two. It's nothing! He's my dad's best friend… and our teacher."

"That wouldn't stop me." They both said in unison and I rolled my eyes at them, turning around, ready to leave the washroom.

"What? It's true. Half of our class is drooling over him. Both guys and girls. I'm sure he already has a secret fan club."

We discussed more fan club theories about James over their burrito bowls and my chicken salad lunch that James had packed for me. It made me smile because I loved his cooking and how he could make something like quinoa taste so delicious.

* * *

"Are you sure about this, Mia?" Aaron asked, raising his brows and handing me two one-hundred-dollar bills. I swallowed the lump in my throat and nodded.

"I'm sure. I'll help you out, don't worry." I pocketed the money and tried my best to hide my shaking hands. "See you in class."

I quickened my pace and headed straight towards the washroom to splash my face with cold water. I had to do it. I couldn't pay my dad's bills with a few thousand dollars. I'd need a few more grands for his bill, and his recovery and medication when he would come back home.

Taking a deep breath, I straightened myself and heard the bell ring for the last class of the day. Lucky for me, it was Design and Colors, *his* class. I fiddled, holding the gift box in my hand.

It will give you multiple O's.

Biting my lips, I stared at the vibrator. If this tiny thing made me cum, I wouldn't need to beg James ever again. Hell, I could put up a show for him and watch him stare at me with his mouth open.

"Fuck it," I muttered, cleaning the vibe and locking myself in the cubicle. Lowering my thong and lifting my skirt, I pressed the silicone against my sex. I whimpered and covered my mouth to muffle it as I pushed the vibrator inside me, my walls stretching with a hint of pain to accommodate its girth.

With another push and a whimper, it settled inside me, leaving only the string out. I straightened up and my eyes widened at the heavy but comfortable feeling of something inside me. It felt snug and tight. I cleaned up and straightened my clothes, hurrying to the classroom. My legs were wobbling by the time I had sat down on my desk. I was sure my cheeks were red too, but I tried to hide them with my hair.

James started the class by asking about our updates for the three trials of paper he had asked us to cut, then he continued teaching about lines. Halfway through the class, I had an intense urge to go to the washroom and pull out the damn vibrator because I was sure I had soaked my entire thong and skirt, and made a puddle on the seat. I was wet and hearing James' voice so close while he looked so fucking hot in glasses and tousled hair made me clench on the vibe.

I couldn't stop myself from squirming in the seat and try to get some friction when I remembered it was remote controlled. I quickly shook off the idea knowing I was in class, and even I didn't have enough guts to use a remote-controlled vibe sitting in a class.

"Take notes and if you have questions, you can ask me after the video has ended." The room darkened, and a video was being played on the screen.

What notes? I scrambled to open a notebook and hold a pen when the video started. I tried to even my breathing and focus on the video that talked about the history of colors and how it… it… *oh, fuck me. This was getting too much.*

I shifted again, and something fell near me, but before I could look down, James was there.

"Are you okay, Mia?" he asked in a low voice, his hot breath brushing over my ear. It was dark and I couldn't make out his features. "You look distracted today. Is everything okay?"

You see, Mister James, my friends gave me this early birthday gift called a vibrating egg, and I thought it would be a great idea to shove it up my pussy before your class started. So, yes, I'm distracted because I'm ready to burst and have my first orgasm in a fucking classroom, so it's all jolly!

"I-It's nothing."

He hummed and leaned down to pick up something that must have fallen. Maybe a pen. One of my pens? I licked my lips and focused on the video and *not* his musky pine scent or how good his ass looked in his tight slacks.

"You've got some fucking guts, you dirty fucking girl." I

froze, hearing his rough voice whisper in my ear. Fear gripped me when he didn't add anything to it and walked away without looking back at me.

What the hell was his problem?

The video ended, and I frowned at his harsh expression when he asked a question.

"What do you think, Miss Miller?" I met his eyes, and they were cold, icy blue.

"About the color theory or…" I trailed off, but I was saved by the bell.

"See me after class." His words rang through me as if he had purred them in my ear with his stern tone.

I sighed and packed my bag. I'd just have to talk to him and then remove the vibe. I hoped he'd hurry up whatever he wanted to scold me about. I stayed at my desk while my classmates who had a few questions talked to James. My hand clenched on the pen I was holding as I saw how close Claire leaned towards him, twirling her perfect wavy golden hair and batting her lashes at him. She even giggled when he explained the color wheel.

My stomach clenched at the sight of them so close, and I hated myself for feeling jealous when I shouldn't. It was wrong, but… I didn't want James to give his full attention to Claire or anyone else but me.

As if sensing my gaze, he glanced in my direction and his face hardened. So he would smile and laugh at Claire but won't offer me the same? *Fine.* I rolled my eyes at him and packed up my notes and stationery. Remembering the remote of the vibe, I made sure it was in the gift box, but when I opened it sneakily… it was empty.

Where the hell was the remote control of my vibrator?

You've got some fucking guts, you dirty fucking girl. James' words clicked into place and my stomach fell when I met his stony gaze. The class was empty except for the two of us.

I held my breath as if I was waiting for an impact.

"Looking for this, Princess?" he asked, his voice low as he held up the tiny black thing with two buttons.

He was holding the remote control of my vibrator.

Fuck me, indeed.

PART III

"Bend over the desk, Princess.
It's time for your punishment"

16

NAUGHTY BRAT

MIA

I pursed my lips and thought about the choices I had.

Option A: I can pretend and lie that I didn't know what the heck that was, but the chances of James catching my lie were pretty high.

Option B: Die from mortification. Unfortunately, it wasn't plausible in the current condition I was in.

Option C: I could nod. Let him scold me for using a sex toy during school, especially his class, and weep in my room for a couple of weeks before changing my name and moving to another country. I've heard Europe's pretty cool about sex toys and walking naked, right?

Option D: Make a run for it. Yeet out of the class. I was highly considering sliding open the window and jumping down from the two-story floor, but I feared breaking my bones and then paying for the hospital bills.

So I had only one chance of escaping.

The door.

I slowly stood up from the chair and heard the students talking loudly in the hallway, clearing their lockers and leaving for home, or some of them, like Summer, were going to detention. While I was stuck in a classroom with a scary hot teacher who I have a dirty crush on, who's also my dad's best friend.

Keeping my head down, I walked by his desk and held my breath as if he was a bear sniffing his prey to see if it was alive or not. I really didn't want James to bite me.

Well... maybe I did, but not in that context.

"Lock the door."

I almost jumped and screeched at his deep sound of his voice. I couldn't meet his eyes. I took a deep breath before clutching the hem of my skirt and walked towards the door. My only chance at escape. Somehow, the vibe inside me felt bigger, and I was confused why my brain and body found the situation I was in extremely hot.

Yep. There's definitely something wrong with my head.

"I won't repeat myself, Mia." James said, still standing by his desk. "Lock the fucking door."

"I... I have to—"

"No. You don't."

Fuck. Me. His voice was scary.

My hand wrapped around the knob of the door, the cool metal making me feel heated. I could run. I wanted to run. But my feet wouldn't follow the commands of my brain. They weren't moving.

I shivered and clenched the handle when a low thrum of vibrations started from the toy. My knees buckled, and I wanted to crawl and remove it because—

"Lock the door and come here." I heard James say from the fog of lust. I was surprised that I could still stand.

The door closed with an echoing click that made me whimper. I was alone. With James. Not the funny, charming James. No, he was scary, angry, teacher-James. I made a sound from my throat and covered my mouth at my embarrassment, pressing my forehead against the wood when he increased the vibrations.

Stupid, stupid, stupid. I just had to keep the fucking remote in my pocket and forget about it. Only if I hadn't—

"Ohmfgh," I muffled my moan and clenched my legs together. I turned around to see the monster who was enjoying my torment. *"Please."*

He pressed a button.

I knelt on the floor, trying to cup myself and stop the thrumming vibrations that were wreaking delicious havoc on my pussy. "Please, James," I choked out through the gasps as tears burned in my eyes. "I... I—*please*."

I was ignored.

He pressed the button again that sent me wailing, crying out in my palm because I didn't know what was happening to me. Sweat gathered on the back of my neck and slid down my back. I was in between places. On one hand, I felt like I was going to pee and die in front of James, and on the other hand, I felt so fucking good as if I was in a heaven and wanted to fly.

"Please, please, please," I begged, but he didn't listen, turning the toy to its highest setting that had my body shaking. I clawed on the floor, trying to hold on to something, but there was nothing. I was going to die.

"Please, Daddy," I cried out.

I heard a chuckle, and the pattern of the vibrations changed.

"Ohmygod." I shivered, and I didn't care anymore. I hated him. I hated the man. I wasn't going to last if he kept his antics. I did the only thing I could do. Yanking my skirt up, I slid my hand down my completely soaked underwear and tried to find the string—

My hand was tugged off and through the blurry haze of my vision, I saw blue. A plea of a whimper rolled out of me.

His hand tightening on my wrist as James raked his gaze over my sprawled body on the classroom floor. I wondered how I looked through his eyes. Kneeling on the floor with my quivering body, the skirt tugged up, panties soaked and ready to explode in pleasure.

"Pretty slut," he whispered, rubbing his thumb over my pulse and my skin singed where he touched me. That one little touch made me want to crawl towards him and wrap myself around his leg and beg him to hold me when I cum. "Are you about to cum?"

I nodded.

"*Mhmm?* Is my princess slut going to orgasm for the first time?" he purred, his delicious voice making me clench on the vibrator that made the pleasure rock through my body.

I knew it was about to happen. I was so close, I could taste it. I wanted to taste it.

"Yes, Daddy."

"Such a good princess," he crooned and pressed another button.

Just as I thought I was about to orgasm—everything paused. All the vibrations stopped and I let out a sob, trying to lift my hip for more vibrations because my orgasm was ripped away from me.

I was so, so close.

"Please! Let me cum. I was so close." I didn't care that I was whining for an orgasm from my teacher on a classroom floor. I wanted to cum so badly. "*Please.*"

James let my wrist go and trailed his fingers from my arm to my neck, slowly patting my cheek. "There, there, sweetheart."

I held his hand and blinked through the frustrated tears, "Please Daddy. Let me cum. Start the vibrations again."

His face darkened when he knelt across me, his sharp, handsome face inches away from me. "Bad girls like you don't get orgasms, Mia. You used a sex toy in my classroom. Tried to play around with its remote while I was teaching and made me repeat myself three times." His tone was soft but firm. His hand wrapped around my jaw when I looked away and pulled me closer.

I squirmed when he glared at me. "Now tell me, you naughty brat, do you deserve an orgasm or a punishment?"

17

I'LL DO ANYTHING

JAMES

I glared at her pretty green eyes as they gleamed with tears. I was truly a sadist to find the sight of her crying so fucking beautiful. I wanted to lean down and capture her pouty mouth with a kiss and punish her for her actions.

Her lips trembled, and I knew she was still shaking from the vibrations of the toy that was buried deep inside her pussy. *Fuck*. I wanted to be the one who gave her first orgasm, bury my fingers inside her, stretch her little cunt and make her cum with my mouth, my cock.

I was jealous of a fucking sex toy.

"Answer me, Princess," I asked again, my tone soft as her body calmed down from the edge, returning to Earth.

As much as I'd love for her to have multiple orgasms through the tiny toy, I wanted to make it comfortable for her. And I was sure she didn't plan to have her first orgasm on a classroom floor.

She could have that bent over my desk.

"I..." Mia licked her lips, her eyes dropping to my lips

before meeting my eyes again. "I'll do anything you want, Daddy."

Shock and surprise coursed through my body, hearing her. Then pure desire, lust, and possessiveness took over. *She was mine.*

"Say that again, Princess," I growled, pulling her closer with an arm around her waist. "Say it."

Her tiny fingers clenched over my shirt as she shifted on my lap and blinked at me through her long, dark lashes. "I'll do anything you want. Please, Daddy."

Mine.

"Even kiss me?" I asked, moving my hand to cup her cheek and wipe a tear from the corner of her eye. I leaned down and licked the trail of tears on her cheek. Kissing her soft skin, I pulled back and whispered, "Would you kiss me if I asked you to?"

"Yes." She took a shaky breath and nodded. "Yes, please, James. I want to kiss you."

I swiped my thumb over her bottom lip and my cock pressed against the confines of my slacks when she parted her lips. I gazed at her, sliding my thumb inside her warm, wet mouth. Her eyes were on me the entire time she sucked and licked my thumb as if it was my dick. Swirling her little tongue and licking it as if it was her personal candy.

Fuck. Me. This girl will be the end of me.

My eyes narrowed at the little temptress when she bit my thumb. I pulled back and lightly held her chin. "I've decided what I'm gonna do with a naughty brat like you."

"What's that, Mister James?" Mia batted her lashes, making herself comfortable on my lap, her cheeks flushing with the prettiest shade of pink.

"I'm going to punish you, Princess."

I pulled away and stood up. Even though her dilated pupils dropped at the bulge on my pants that was just across her mouth, I kept my tone firm despite how much I wanted to wrap my hand around her hair and push her face against the zipper, ordering her to use her teeth to tug down the zipper and please me.

"Choose a safe word, Mia."

She took a long time to drift her eyes from the front of my pants to my face. "Safe word?"

"You say that word and everything stops."

Mia frowned as if I had said something absurd. "But I don't want it to stop."

This fucking girl...

I cupped her cheek and caressed her cheekbone, "Sweetheart, you will change your mind about that. Pick a word. For your safety and... my conscience."

"You've a conscience, Daddy?"

I narrowed my eyes and, wrapping a hand around her hair, I tugged hard enough to make her whimper, "I'd watch that little mouth of yours, if I were you, Princess. Pick a word or game's over and you can go home and play with your toy."

She shook her head. "No, no, I... I'll say peach."

"Peach?" I loosened my hold on her hair and raked my hand through it. "Are you sure?"

"Very sure." Mia squirmed and licked her lips, looking at me with such a hopeful smile that makes me want to rip out my heart for her. *Scary*. It was scary how much I was willing to do for her... and to her.

"Can we please start now, Daddy?"

Mia

I gazed up at James, still on my knees, when he smiled down at me. My body trembled seeing it. It was anything but a happy, hopeful smile. It was wicked and mischievous.

Licking my lips, I waited eagerly for his next command. I would do just about anything he would tell me to.

"Greedy slut," he murmured, lightly tugging a lock of my hair before pulling away. "Already begging Daddy for a punishment."

My walls tightened around the toy, a jolt of pleasure rolling through my body hearing his smoky, velvety voice. I didn't know why, but I enjoyed it when he called me that.

"Stand up and come here, Princess," James said, leaning against his desk, his long legs spread out as he watched my every move like a predator. Before I could straighten up, he shook his head, stopping me. "I changed my mind. I want you to crawl here."

Heat burned my cheeks as I flickered my eyes at the floor and the distance between me and the desk. *Why the hell am I already considering crawling towards him?*

"Crawl?"

"You were a bad girl today, a naughty fucking brat and crawling on the floor would be the least of your worries, Princess." James crossed his arms, his expression darkening. "Crawl, or say the safe word, Mia."

Taking a deep breath, I moved my hair over my shoulder and pressed my hands on the floor. Shame and humiliation burn through my veins. Still, my underwear dampened with each move.

"Look at me when you crawl."

My knees pressed against the hard floor and I stared up at him, holding onto his dark, piercing gaze. Watching him watch me. Somehow, even on my knees, crawling for him, I felt powerful and confident. Because he looked at me as if I was everything he desired and *more*. Raking his eyes from my face to neck, to the arch of my back and the curve of my ass and the bare skin of my legs. His jaw twitched, and I wanted to see him unravel for me.

"Do you enjoy seeing me crawl for you, Daddy?" I asked, my voice sultry as I swayed my hips and arched my back. I wanted to see him snap. To punish me, like he promised me he would.

His blue eyes gleamed with lust as he answered, "Of course I do, my naughty princess slut."

When I neared him, he leaned down to cup my cheek, and I almost nuzzled my face in his hand. He always touched me so tenderly, so gently. As much as I adored it, I wanted to see his strength.

"If I could, I'd keep you on a leash and order you to crawl everywhere."

"L-leash?" My eyes widened when he smirked and straightened up.

"Don't worry your pretty little head about it. Bend over the desk, Princess. It's time for your punishment."

I took a shaky breath when I stood up, my legs trembling as I felt the toy shift inside me. "I-I want to remove the—*oh.*"

James didn't let me finish. At one moment, I was standing, and the second, I was bent over the desk with my cheek pressed hard against the wood. I squirmed, feeling more arousal seep out of me.

"Quit moving." The hold of his hand on the back of my neck tightened. "Or it'll hurt more."

Hurt? I didn't like being hurt. I didn't want to be hurt. I didn't want him to hurt me out of all the people.

"I-I, James… *wait—*"

A gasp escaped my throat when a spank was delivered to my ass. Its sharp sting burned and a moment later, it spread all over my body and I was getting wetter.

What the hell?

"I'm going to teach you an important lesson today, Princess."

"W-what's that Daddy?"

I whimpered when his entire length pressed against me, his body covering mine, his hot breath tickling the shell of my ear as he whispered in his deep, smoky voice,

"Don't let your mouth write a check your ass can't cash, Princess."

18

YOU TASTE LIKE HEAVEN

MIA

Biting my lip, I wriggled my ass, trying to feel his hardened length closer to where I needed him. But I ached everywhere, my body thrumming with the need to be filled, touched, kissed, licked. Whatever adverbs or adjectives there were to perform bodily intimacy with each other.

The soft pads of his fingers brushed over the backs of my thighs, making me shiver. I took a deep breath, trying to control the aching need bubbling inside me. They slid over my inner thigh, gliding over to my ass. I stayed still, wishing he'd never stop when I felt the slight shake of his breathing.

Was he turned on by this as much as I was?

No, it could be that he didn't like the plain white underwear I wore.

Before I could voice out my worry, he cupped my ass and squeezed. Hard. "You've a fucking lovely ass." I took a sharp breath when he slapped one of my cheek, keeping the skirt flipped over my back. "I'm going to turn it into the perfect shade of pink so you remember your punishment every time you sit. Would you like that, Princess?"

I looked over my shoulder and nodded, meeting his cloudy gaze. My lips parted into a soundless gasp when he spanked me again, my body rocking on the desk and leaning on my toes to feel some sort of comfort.

"Use your words, big girl," he cooed, smoothening the burning sting on my ass. "You can use your tongue, can't you, Princess?"

"Y-yes, Daddy."

"Mhmm. Maybe I'll use your mouth for a punishment next time."

Next time? My mouth?

My fingers tightened on the edge of the desk, trying to hold on to something because I had an idea of what was about to come next. I looked over my shoulder to find his perfect, long fingers wrapping around the sides of my thong and pulling it up, stretching it over my ass. I whimpered when the lace pressed over my sensitive clit.

"That felt good, Princess?"

"Y-Yes, it did." I licked my lips and added, "I want you to touch me."

James clucked his tongue. "Already begging for a touch and we haven't even started the punishment yet, Princess." He tapped my thigh. "Spread your legs. More." *Smack*. I gasped, feeling the stinging burn on my thigh. "I know you can spread them wider—*thattagirl*."

Oh, fuck, the punishment was getting harder and harder and he hadn't even started—

"*Ow!*" The burning sting was sharper and more painful. "It hurts!"

He soothed the burn on my cheek with his fingers, warmth spreading over my pussy, and I had to hold myself from leaning back on his touch.

"It's supposed to hurt, Princess. It's a punishment." James pulled back and asked, "What's your safe word?"

"Peach."

"Do you want to use it?"

I stayed silent and slowly shook my head, clutching the desk until my knuckles turned white. "No, Daddy."

My entire body jumped when he spanked another cheek with the same intensity and murmured, "Good girl. Now, start counting each spank and tell me you're sorry."

I frowned and looked over at him, "That wasn't the part of de—*ow*."

He interrupted me with another smack. His eyes were hard to read when he said, "The longer you wait, the longer your ass will be punished. If your little ass gets bruised sooner, I will move to your pussy. Then your tits. Until you beg me like a good girl. Understood?"

My answer was quick and breathy. "Yes, Daddy. Understood."

He repeated his actions, the muscles of my calves tensing with the strike. "O-one. I'm sorry, Daddy."

Spank.

"Sorry for what?"

"I-I… for being a bad girl and using a sex toy."

Spank.

"Repeat again."

I pressed my teeth on my bottom lip and trembled. "I'm sorry for being a bad girl and using a sex toy in your class, Daddy."

His voice softened, and he rewarded me with a 'Good girl' and a soothing rub on my burning cheek.

In a few moments, my eyes became half-lidded as I kept my gaze on the white wall with my cheek on the wooden desk, my mouth answering each spank with an apology. My body was floating in a strange dimension where pain started feeling like pleasure. With each spank, I moved my hips back, asking—*begging* for more. As much as I craved for the smack of his palm, I thirsted for the little moments when he'd rub my bruising skin and praise me with a loving, 'Good girl' or a rare 'Good Princess.'

"P-please," I cried out when the slow vibrations started. "I-I'll…"

"Shh, Princess," he hushed me, delivering another spank, but it felt different from before because of the toy. "You can handle it. You'll remember not to use sex toys in the class. Especially during your dad's bestfriend's class, the one who makes your pussy so fucking wet. Isn't that right, my sweet princess slut?"

"Yes, Daddy," I moaned, his fingers tracing the hem of my thong. "Please touch me."

He paused and opened a drawer, closing it after a few moments. The vibrations increased, and I held on to the desk for my dear life. My legs were trembling when something cold and flat touched the backs of my knees.

"What's your safe word, Princess?" he asked, his voice threateningly soft that made the hair on the back of my neck raise.

"*Peach*," I breathed out. "What are you doing?"

"Punishing my naughty fucking brat," he answered, and what followed was a sharp sound of something hard slapping against the burning skin of my ass. It *hurt*. The previous spanks were nothing compared to the one he had just—

"It hurts." I let out a soft moan, trying to soothe the burn with my hand, but he held my wrist at my lower back, pinning me to his desk. I looked over his shoulder to see him holding a wooden ruler that he used to teach us during the class. Seeing him use it to spank me, punish me, made me feel embarrassed and hot at the same time.

"Four more, Princess." James soothed the stinging burn that made the warmth pool in my underwear, and the vibrations inside me shook me to the pleasure world. "Can you handle it?"

"I don't know." Tears were threatening to spill, and I was feeling bad for thinking rashly and using a toy in the class.

I felt him take a step back, and I instantly missed the warmth he provided. "Keep your hands where they are or you'll get hurt."

"Yes, Daddy."

I braced myself for the impact, anticipation making it scarier yet exciting. *Smack. Smack. Smack.* I whimpered, covering my mouth to hide the groan and squeezing my eyes shut. I was leaning on the top of my toes and my body trembled with the pain and pleasure rocking through it.

"Such a good girl," James praised me, "Only one left, Princess."

I nodded and took a shaky breath—

"Daddy," I cried out when he spanked me for the last time, my knees buckling as I tipped over the edge.

Warm hands soothed and rubbed the red skin, covering me in a gentle caress and turning me around. Through the haze of my pain and pleasure, I heard him whisper sweet praises in my ears, holding me against his chest and letting me curl on his lap when he sat down on the chair.

"How do you feel, sweet girl?" he asked, brushing my hair out of my face and peering down at me.

The vibrations had stopped, and I felt empty without it. "I want to cum," I said, shifting on his lap so I could straddle him, biting my lip when I felt the hard bulge. I met his gaze and felt the intense lust that also reflected in my eyes.

"You want to cum like this?" he asked, trailing his hands over my body. "Don't want to use your pretty fingers to make yourself cum? Or the little toy that's inside your pussy?"

I shook my head, rocking my hips back and forth,

wondering if I was doing okay. His jaw clenched and hands tightened on my waist. "I want you to make me cum, Daddy."

"I can feel how soaked you are, Princess," he whispered, his eyes trailing from where I was grinding on top of him to my face. He smiled, cupping my cheek. "Look at you."

I didn't understand what he said. I just wanted him to touch me.

"Will you touch my pussy?"

"This dirty mouth will get you in trouble someday." His blue eyes darkened, his thumb pressing on my bottom lip. "And haven't I taught you manners? Do you want more punishment?"

I licked his thumb and peered at him. "Please touch my pussy, Daddy?"

I didn't think James would do it, but he squeezed my ass, making me whimper at the sharp gust of pain. He lifted me as if I was light as a feather and put me down on the desk. The cold wood stung against my bruised skin. *So this is what he meant, that I'll remember the punishment for a few days.*

"Whose pussy is it, Princess?" he asked, spreading my knees and stepping closer, the bulge in his pants prominent.

I licked my lips and glanced at his face. "Y-yours, Daddy."

He tsked. "Say it."

I swallowed the lump in my throat and whispered, "It's your pussy, Daddy." Arousal burned through my pussy and I clenched the toy that still felt bigger than ever inside me, making me hornier.

"That's right." He cupped me through the thong and squeezed, whispering against my lips, "This is my cunt, Princess. You don't get to play with it unless I let you, understood?"

"But—"

"I'll make you cum. But I want it on my orders." James pulled back his hand and licked his fingers, making me blush.

He hadn't even touched me yet. I had soaked through the underwear to wet his finger. "You taste like heaven, Princess."

"What are you doing?" I asked when he pulled away. He should have been kissing me.

"I promised you I'd take you out today before you decided to misbehave." He checked his expensive watch and held up his open palm at me. "Give me your panties."

"Why?" I crossed my arms.

He tilted his head and pulled out a black controller from his pocket. "Do you really want to test me when I have the controller of the vibrating toy that's inside your pussy?"

I swallowed the lump in my throat and shook my head, wincing as I straightened up from the desk. Handing him my soaked thong felt naughty yet arousing. He quickly pocketed it, and, stepping closer, he pressed a kiss to my forehead.

"Good girl. Do you trust me to take care of you, Princess?"

I blinked at his rubbish question and nodded quickly. "Of course I do, James."

He had a strange emotion in his eyes as he slowly nodded. "Good. Then I'll take care of you. Keep your cunt bare until I say so."

19
THAT GOES UP THE BUTT

MIA

"Are we really going to a sex store?" I asked, looking out of the car window.

Even though I was pouting because I still hadn't felt what an orgasm felt like, James told—*nay*, ordered me to clean up in the washroom and remove the vibe and put it back in the box. When I complained that I didn't want to, he threatened to remove it by himself and punish my pussy with spanks.

Despite how turned on I got by the idea, I obeyed and cleaned up.

It was a sunny, warm day and James had turned on the air conditioner in his car.

"I already answered that question the first couple of times you asked me, Mia," he replied, squeezing my thigh. He had kept his hand on my thigh as soon as we had driven out of the school, as if he couldn't stop touching me and making silly little patterns on my skin with his fingers.

It made my heart feel all warm and mushy.

I squirmed on the seat, trying to hide the wince of pain. I remembered checking out my ass in the washroom, blushing at the sight of a red hue spread all over my cheeks. Despite using a wonder ruler to spank me, James hadn't bruised me once and it must've taken him practice learning how to spank. Which meant, he had done it before. He had spanked someone before and the thought of that had made my mouth bitter.

I didn't want him to spank anyone else than me.

Keeping my hand on his knuckles, I glanced at him, at the little smile curling on the corner of his lips, and looked away when a blush crept up my neck and ears.

As long as James was with me, I didn't need to worry. He had promised me he'd stay.

James kept his promises.

* * *

"That goes up the butt."

I jumped, almost dropping the box I was holding, turning around to meet the green eyes of a guy who looked a few years older than me with inky black hair. He smiled and pointed to the box I was gripping to my chest as if to protect myself from an attack.

"I figured that out. It says, 'Heart-Shaped Three-Inch Butt Plug for Anal Play,' after all." I read the badge on his black shirt and said his name, "Nate. Uh, I'm not interested in this. Thank you, though."

He gladly accepted the box that had a huge photo of a glass butt plug and kept it on the shelf. "That's okay. But it is something fun if you ever want to try. With lots of lube." His eyes twinkled, flashing me a sly smirk. He nodded at the other toys that looked similar to the butt plug I was checking out to fuel my curiosity. "For beginners, I highly recommend starting from a small one and get used to the feeling of something—"

"She said," a strong arm wrapped around me, pressing me against the warm chest as a low voice rumbled through him, "she's not interested in this."

Nate and James shared a macho eye contact, and I felt like diving into a pit, covering myself. I cleared my throat and tried to pull away from James, but his arm was like a metal band, keeping me glued to him.

"I was introducing her to the wonders of—"

"If there's any introduction to be done, I'll be the one to do that, *kid*," James replied, smiling at him in a way that was taunting, emphasizing the word 'kid' even though Nate looked like he was in college.

His eyes danced between the two of us, his smirk widening. "Sure thing, *Dad*."

My cheeks burned at his taunt and I would've chopped my arm off for an invisibility cloak at the moment. "I'll be at the counter if you need any help. Cock cages are on aisle six and leashes are on aisle nine. Tootles!"

"I want to kill him," James whispered underneath his breath as soon as Nate walked away, at least out of our earshot.

"Calm down, papa bear." I patted his chest and walked over to the cock cages as Nate had said and picked a lilac pink one. It was made of metal and had a weird but cute heart shaped lock at the bottom where I guess balls are supposed to be. It looked scary, more of a contraption than a sex toy. Shuddering, I put it down, wondering why and exactly who would buy something like that.

"It's for chastity, Princess." My eyes drifted towards him, his fingers trailing over the other belt like thing which had a heart cutout at the front and locks at the bottom. He smirked at me and said, "They have one for naughty girls who can't keep their hands to themselves."

My throat felt dry. Licking my lips, I asked, "W-why would anyone buy it though?"

"It's a kink. Staying in denial after edging and giving the control to their partner."

"But why would anyone do that?" I frowned, touching the leather of the belt he was looking at. It seemed expensive, but I didn't understand the use of padlocks. "Isn't orgasm the end goal?"

He chuckled and stepped closer to me, my back against his hard chest, his arm loosely wrapped around me. I shivered when his hand trailed over the inner thigh, reminding me I was not wearing any underwear.

"James."

He clucked his tongue, pinching me, making me gasp and bite my bottom lip.

"D-Daddy," I corrected, trying to wriggle away, but his arm tightened.

"I've been edging you all this time, Princess. Keeping you denied," he whispered in my ear, shivers spiraling over my entire body. To others, we would look like a couple in an embrace, but I precisely felt the small teasing touches and caresses of his fingers over my inner thigh, slowly inching closer to where I throbbed. "You're already into it, as far as I can tell."

"B-but I wanted to orgasm each time."

"I know, sweet girl." He kissed my neck and cupped my pussy, moving his fingers over my slick entrance. "But you couldn't, could you? You need Daddy's help to orgasm. His fingers, his mouth, his cock, *hm?*"

I nodded, trying to hold still and not grind myself against his hand that felt so, so good touching my clit. "I need you, Daddy."

"I know, Princess," James groaned, kissing the soft skin below my ear, his hot breath tickling me. "I know."

A whimper escaped my lips when he pulled away, tucking the hem of my skirt to my thigh. I turned around to find him licking his fingers with a dark expression on his face.

"Why'd you stop?"

"Because I didn't want my little princess slut to orgasm for the first time in a sex toy shop, where everyone can hear her sweet moans," he answered, fixing the rolled-up sleeves of his shirt. My cheeks burned, and I looked around to make sure we were alone when he added, "And don't talk to Nate again."

Huh? Why shouldn't I talk to the employee? Nate seemed fine and—

"Get anything you want. If you behave." He leaned down and whispered in my ear, "We can use those toys next time we play." Kissing my cheek, he pulled back and walked to another aisle that had hanging chains and scarier looking equipment.

I shuddered and started browsing through the vibrators and dildos sections. If I had told Emma and Summer about James, I don't think they would be surprised that he was spoiling me with delicious spanking punishments and buying me expensive sex toys.

Maybe I *should* start calling him my Sugar Daddy. *Ha.*

20
I WANT TO KNOW YOU

JAMES

"If you keep sighing like that, you'll get wrinkles early," Mia commented.

I glanced at Mia, who shouldn't look adorable in a messy bun and a baggy band tee shirt. I hadn't thought twice about buying any toys or lingerie she wanted at the sex shop and kept my glare fixated on Nate's dark hair when he had scanned all her items, humming a tune. Mia had been a little upset about me paying everything for her, but I was her caregiver for a few days. I would buy her a yacht if she asked me to, and I wouldn't blink an eye.

Maybe it is time to go talk to my therapist again, because I was sure that my behavior wasn't normal when it came to a certain doe-eyed minx.

"Do I look like someone who cares about wrinkles, Princess?" I muttered, looking back at the blueprints, eyeing the dimensions and going through the various excel sheets wondering what I was missing.

We had dinner, and she was doing her homework on the kitchen island while I was going through the designs on my laptop for a new club that my PA was working on.

Despite the sexual tension hovering between us, both of us worked in comfortable silence with a few soft hums coming from her as she nodded along to songs she listened to on her earphones.

"I know you don't care, but I do. So, unless you want to wear a sheet mask tonight before you sleep, stop sighing." She was scolding me but instead, she looked extremely adorable. "Why are you sighing anyway?"

"Come here and help me pick a product." She quickly stood up and walked towards my chair and I pulled her on my lap, inhaling her sweet cherry scent, and showed her the screen of the laptop. "This is purple damask wallpaper and this is red and black vinyl wallpaper. Which one do you think will suit this room?"

Her eyes were wide and glittery as she squinted at the three-dimensional model of the room and aped at me. "Is that a pole?"

"Yes."

"In middle of the bedroom?"

"Uh-huh."

Mia turned towards me with a raised brow and scarlet color tinting her cheeks. "What exactly are you making here?"

"It's a secret." I pinched her waist and nodded at the screen. "Help me choose a wallpaper."

"I like the purple one but don't tell me you were sighing about wallpaper for the past ten minutes."

"Will you believe me if I said I was?"

She blinked and said, "No."

I smiled, dipping down and brushing my lips over her ear, enjoying the way she trembled. "Good girl." I pulled back and said, "I have to choose the lighting, jacuzzi, shower and…" I couldn't certainly tell her about *that* so I kept it simple, "Some furniture for the room."

Mia sensed my hesitation. "What kind of furniture?"

I patted her ass and she stood up, "I'll show you once you finish your homework."

Poking her tongue at me, she watched me type for a few moments before asking, "Can I ask you a question?"

"You just asked." I paused seeing her face and tilted my head. "Ask away, Princess."

"Why did you decide to take this job?" She fidgeted with her fingers before adding, "Teaching, I mean."

Partly because I want to keep an eye on you knowing half of the school board is corrupt and partly because…

"Clyde helped me finish school, did you know that?" By her stunned expression and wide eyes, I would take it she didn't. "I wanted to drop out but he was a stubborn piece of ass—still is, and helped me. I've already travelled half of the world working on onsite projects and saved enough to do whatever the hell I want, so I decided to accept this teaching contract." I looked back at the blueprints and smiled, "I like lines, colors, dimensions and space. The ability to create, build something monumental or something just for others gives me thrill. And I want to share this knowledge to others."

When I glanced back at Mia, she was smiling. My body stiffened seeing it. It was pure, innocent and otherworldly. I didn't know how to react and kept staring at her. She was beautiful.

"I'm glad you decided to teach us," she said, leaning down and brushing a kiss on my cheek before settling herself on her seat and continuing her homework.

I rubbed my chest, exhaling the breath I was holding. She was going to ruin me.

After a few moments, she looked up again and I knew she was curious. Again.

"Can I ask you about something?"

"What is it?" I asked.

Mia nibbled on her lower lip. "You've never talked to me about your family." My face must have been a dead giveaway why I didn't, as she quickly scrambled to add, "I mean, it's okay if you don't want to. It's just... it's odd that I never knew your mom was a chef until last week."

I closed my laptop and leaned back on the chair, crossing my arms. "Why is that odd, Mia?"

Her cheeks flushed under my gaze and she cleared her throat before opening her mouth. "You know everything about me. About my family, my dad, my mom..." She blinked quickly because I knew if she didn't, she'd cry. "How she... you know." *I know, Princess.* I clenched my fist, hiding the urge to haul her over my lap and rub her back. "You even know my friends and teach them. You know I hate eggplants and you still cooked a dish that made me like them!"

She wasn't making any sense.

Yet, I understood her.

"I want to know about you. Not just your job, the car you drive, the suits you wear or what type of women you like in your bed." She looked down at her open notes of AP Chemistry. "I want to know you, James."

My jaw ticked thinking about everything I couldn't tell her because if I did, she would hate me. She would never see me the same way with her twinkling hazel-green eyes that made my stomach clench. Because whenever she looked at me, I felt more alive than I have ever been for the past thirty-five years of my life. I felt seen.

And because I was a selfish son of a bitch who only cared about himself and his success, I smiled cruelly at her, "You know everything that I want you to know about me, Princess."

My fist tightened as she frowned at me, her eyes dulling. "But... I don't. Why can't you tell me about yourself, James?"

"Because you haven't earned it yet," I said harshly.

She blinked at my sharp tone, and, once again, I pushed down the urge to embrace her in my arms.

"*Earned it yet?* Haven't I earned it?"

God, she sounded so hopeful and sweet.

I hated myself more than anyone at that moment, because I was going to crush her hope.

Leaning my arms on the marble, I kept my eyes on her face and said, "Just because I buy you pretty clothes and sex toys doesn't mean I trust you, Princess."

Mia took a sharp breath, hurt clearly visible on her face. We stared at each other for a few moments, thick silence stretching over us fueled with anger and tension, her fingers clutching the little heart necklace on her chest.

"Of course," she bit out, her face twisting in pure rage. "I'd have to gag on your oh-so-magical-cock to earn your trust, don't I? Or do I earn it by spreading my thighs for you and letting you fuck me while I call you Daddy? Which one is it?"

"Watch your tone, Mia—"

"*No.*" She stood up. "I've had enough. I thought you were different, but no, you are just a sick, perverted old guy who just wants to get in my pants."

She seemed furious, and I didn't blame her. I had acted out of line, but I didn't know how to explain to her why I couldn't open up my heart to her and tell her everything about me.

If I did, I'd lose her.

"*Mia...*" I stood up, removing my glasses. "What are you doing?"

She was mindlessly throwing everything in her duffle bag that I hadn't noticed before. She glared at me, zipping it shut. "I'm not going to stay here and let you belittle me by all that earning your trust nonsense. If you didn't want to answer me, you could've just told me you weren't ready to share and I would've understood. I'm not a fucking kid, James."

"I know you are not a kid," I said, standing up. My stomach twisted and clenched with nerves. It wasn't like I didn't trust her, I did, more than I cared to admit it, but I didn't want to open up to her. I was afraid of her hating me. Leaving me and crying on her friends' shoulders, cursing me and never meeting my eyes again. I had lost too many important people in my life, I couldn't lose her too.

She turned around and seethed, "Then tell me, or at least stop treating me like one."

I didn't reply. I couldn't. Seeing her so mad at me for the first time, I didn't know how and where to start. Especially when her eyes closed off, and I knew she was pulling away. I couldn't do anything but watch when she picked up the bag and wore her Vans.

"Where are you going, Mia?" I asked, my tone cold, closing the door before she could leave.

"Why should I tell you?" She asked, "You don't care."

I took a step closer and loomed over her. "Trust me, little Princess, if there's one person I care more about myself in this entire world, it's you. So watch your fucking tone and tell me where you are going because I will not let you put yourself in danger just because you're mad at me."

Her eyes were gleamed with tears as she whispered, "I'm going to Emma's house for a sleepover." Mia looked away, her shaking hands clutching the duffle bag. "I'll call a cab."

"Like hell you will," I answered and pulled away to calm myself. Because if she cried or even a single tear fell from her eyes, I was going to lose it and lock her with me until we both calmed down enough to have a conversation about my past. "I'll drop you off. Stay here."

I trusted her enough not to run away when I went upstairs into her room. Picking the thing I was looking for, I came back and sighed internally to see her waiting for me at the front door. Even mad, she didn't want to disappoint me.

Her eyes lit up a little when I handed her the elephant stuffy she couldn't sleep without. She clutched it to her chest, and I looked away, tugging at the collar of my shirt.

"Let's go."

* * *

THE RIDE to Emma's house was filled with silence and, unfortunately for both of us, it was full of tension and anger and guilt. Although, the guilt was all over me. I couldn't tell her everything. I couldn't open up about myself just yet. I was a selfish piece of shit who wanted to cling to her for a little more.

She can hate me all she wants after she knows.

"Call me if anything happens," I said, gripping the steering wheel so tight that my knuckles turned pale just so I wouldn't lift my hand and wrap it around her wrist and tell her to wait.

Mia didn't even look at me as she opened the door and stepped out, saying a small "Goodnight."

My jaw clenched as I watched her lithe frame walk past the golden tall gates, even the security guard smiling at her. From the car, I watched someone open the double doors and Mia disappeared into the mansion of Dorothy Moore.

Despite being a school night, I reversed my car and drove to one club where I knew I would find peace among the chaos. I needed a couple of drinks.

21
SHOW ME YOU CARE

MIA

"I think I might be asexual."

Emma paused *Howl's Moving Castle,* and we both turned to Summer who was sprawled on an entire couch by herself, stuffing kernels of popcorn in her mouth. Emma's house was built like a mansion and had its own home theater, where we all were currently sprawled with tons of blankets, pillows, snacks and junk food to last a month.

"Didn't you hook up with an entire football team?" I asked.

"I didn't. It's a rumor."

Emma patted the sheet masks that were on our face and motioned me to remove it. "Then why do you think you might be asexual?"

She shrugged and sat up, staring at her lap and thinking hard. "I don't feel any sexual desire whatsoever towards anyone. Unless it's Howl, of course."

"Of course." Emma and I muttered in unison. Howl and other Ghibli heroes were perfect boyfriend materials.

"Maybe you could be demisexual? Isn't asexuality a spectrum?" I said, patting the serum of the mask all over my face and down my neck. As soon as I had arrived, Emma had ordered me to put on one of her skincare items.

"Could be, and it is." Summer glanced at both of us and smiled. "Thanks guys. I just feel weird that I used to go on so many dates, and I just feel so awkward if anyone hugs me for a second longer."

"Aw, I get that. You don't have to date if you don't want to. Only a few boys in the football team will feel heartbroken."

I nudged my shoulder with her. "How's your favorite quarterback doing?" Caleb was one of the best players in our school football team.

Emma twirled her hair and scowled. "We had a fight, and he's been avoiding me ever since." She sniffed and got comfortable on the couch, patting the side for me to squeeze in. I snuggled with the blanket as she continued, "I know he was wrong, so I'm waiting for him to apologize."

I remembered the small fight I had with James about trust and not having earned it. "How do you know it's not your fault, Em?" I asked and quickly added, "I mean, I'm not taking sides, but what if you both were right and... don't know how to solve it?"

Summer quipped in, "Communication is very important to have a healthy relationship."

"As much as I appreciate your input, neither of you have been in any relationship. Not once," Emma said, and gave me a pointed stare. "If Caleb wanted to talk, he'd try to reach out to me and have a conversation, but he's avoiding my texts and everything. I'll kill him if he doesn't attend your birthday party."

"Oh, no," I groaned, hiding my face in a pillow when I remembered it was the day after tomorrow.

"Oh, yes." Summer grinned and joined us on the couch,

wriggling herself between us and offering the bowl of popcorn. I took a handful. "Did you use the vibrator and had multiple Os?"

I choked and sputtered, but swallowed the food. Both of them were looking at me with wide eyes, and it made me flutter underneath their stare.

"I haven't used it yet," I said, squirming on the couch, feeling the odd sting of spanks. James had laid me across his lap after my shower and applied a generous amount of cold lotion that would heal the bruises so I wouldn't feel sore. He had said such sweet words to me, slowly massaging my skin and praising me and even helping me get dressed, even though I didn't need his help. It was such a caring moment.

But then he turned out to be a pig.

Men.

"I'll let you know when I use it. Thank you for the vibe, by the way," I grinned at both of them, "I know I'll get a lot of use out of it."

Emma played the movie and said, "If you want more toys, let me know."

"Guys," Summer shushed us, "Please let me focus on Howl's cooking skill."

We all hummed in agreement, getting lost in the wondrous world of the movie.

* * *

"Miss Miller." I stiffened and kept my poker face as I lifted my eyes from the paint to meet his blue eyes.

I had avoided his texts ever since he dropped me off for a sleepover. He knew I'd come to school with Em and Summer because Emma had a chauffeur. He looked handsome as ever in one of his crisp shirts, but he was wearing a black one which I hadn't seen him wear before. It suited him, and I hated that it did. Stretching over his shoulders and clinging to his biceps because he had rolled off the sleeves to show off his veiny forearms.

Even his face was freshly shaved and his eyes didn't have any bags underneath them. He didn't look like someone who wanted to apologize for being a giant dick.

I glared at him so hard that I hoped that the sexy glasses he wore would shatter beneath my gaze. But, of course, they didn't. "Yes, Mister James?" I asked, my voice full of sweetness.

"See me after class. I need to discuss something with you."

"I've another class," I lied.

His eyes narrowed, and he said in a stern voice, "It won't take long."

Before I could deny him, he moved on to helping one of my classmates. I glowered and focused all my attention on the empty canvas before me. He had given us free rein to draw and paint whatever we wanted because he was impressed with all of our models. I was going to paint it a soft pastel color to create a beautiful sky with landscape, but my mood had turned sour. I didn't want to talk to him or be alone with him.

"Thank you for waiting, Princess," he said when the last student walked out of the classroom.

"Don't call me that." I crossed my arm and looked at the board over his shoulder. "What is it? I—"

"I know you don't have any class right now." He moved closer until he was standing across from me in front of his desk. "I wanted to... Mia. Look at me."

"I don't want to."

"I can't apologize to you if you won't look at me."

"I don't want to look at you." My lower lip wobbled, and I desperately tried to sound strong, but it came out in a whisper. "You hurt me, James."

"Oh, Princess." Warm hand cupped my cheek, and I finally met his eyes, shocked to see his blue eyes were storming with so many emotions. "I'm sorry, Mia. For hurting you and saying those harsh things that I didn't mean. You don't have to forgive me, but I'm sorry for pushing you away."

"Why did you?" I asked, pressing closer. "You said those hurtful things and told me you didn't trust me. Then you gave me my elephant stuffy that I can't sleep without and told me you care about me. It's confusing me, James."

I saw his throat bob and for a split second I was in awe of his adam's-apple before focusing on what was important.

"Care and trust are two completely different things, Princess." His eyes flickered to my lips. "I care about you. I trust you. But I need time to consider—*Mia*."

"Show me, James." I didn't heed his warning voice and leaned closer. Close enough that there was no distance between us. I licked my lips and tipped on my toes, "Show me you care about me, Daddy."

His eyes widened and once again, I was lost in the way he looked, how scary, intimidating, yet lovely he seemed. "Show you how, Princess?" His voice was rough, and it grated against my spine, goosebumps erupting all over my body that I arched towards him, pressing my breasts against his thin shirt.

We were so close that I could feel his thrumming heartbeat through the layers of fabric between us. That I could feel his warm breath brushing against my cheek. And yet, I wanted more.

Craved it.

"Kiss me." I scrunched my hands on the collar of his shirt and whispered, "Kiss me, Daddy."

His lips parted and my eyes dipped towards them before closing the distance between the two of us, pressing my lips against his. Electricity sparked between us, firing through us as I sighed—finally, finally, *finally*—while he groaned. I moved against him and he pressed closer, my back hitting the edge of his desk while his hands pinned me in place.

A soft moan elicited from my throat that he swallowed greedily and kissed me with a rough passion that was all sweet yet scary at the same time. I wanted more. My hands feathered his soft locks while his wrapped at the back of my neck as if I would ever move away from his kiss.

James was kissing me. And it felt way better than anything I had dreamed of.

22
FORGIVEN YET?

JAMES

Her lips. *Fuck*. Her lips. I breathed and kissed her again and *yes*… there it was again. Her lips tasted like the summer rain. Soft little showers that made the scorching sun bearable in the hot season of May. Her lips were as soft as the wet dew and as addictive as the smell of wet earth.

I wanted to devour her, yet keep her in my arms all the time.

It was maddening.

"Your lips," I groaned, biting her bottom lip until I elicited a satisfying whimper from her, clutching her little fingers on my shirt. "I fucking love how you taste, Princess."

She moaned when I pressed her against the desk, claiming her in a passionate kiss once more. I was eager to spread her out and sample her other set of lips. I grunted, pinning my hips against her, making her aware of how much she affected me.

"James," Mia whimpered, arching her back and curling her fingers on the back of my nape. It felt *so* good. I had forgotten how good it felt.

It wasn't enough. It would never be enough when it came to her.

"Am I forgiven yet?" I purred, trailing my hand down her skirt and lifting it to press against the wet spot between her thighs. "Your pussy thinks so."

"Not yet. *More*," she demanded with a gasp when I licked the soft skin of her neck, placing a small bite. "I want more."

I agreed, nodding against her lips and rubbing her little bundle of nerves as she writhed in my arms, clutching me and caressing me everywhere and all I wanted to do was slide her soaked panties to the side and thrust inside her.

"I'll give you everything," I promised, gazing at her hazel-green eyes that were half lidded with lust. "I'll give you everything and more, Princess. Any fucking thing you want."

"Kiss me." Her lips moved in a breathy whisper and before I could obey her little command, we both heard the footsteps outside the classroom.

Knock knock.

"Mister James. I need to talk." It wasn't a student who needed help with design or understanding color theory. No, it was worse.

The dean.

I moved back and straightened her clothes, fixing the buttons of her shirt because I didn't know when and how I had snuck my hand underneath it to unhook her bra.

"H-how did you—*ugh*," she whispered in panic before clasping the hook. "You're insane."

I patted down her hair before settling in my chair. "You're the one who kissed me, Princess. Now behave." Clearing my throat, I said, "Come in."

Eden Stark entered the room, dressed in a dark dress that suited her, looking like a Bond-villain even when she was in her mid-fifties. Her dark hair was coiled in a bun and through her glasses, her steely grey eyes narrowed when they landed on Mia, who was busy finishing painting her canvas on the front desk. She pretended to not notice the dean until she walked near the desk and widened her eyes.

"Oh, hello, Mrs. Eden."

She ignored her and instead looked at me, crossing her arms. "Isn't the class over?"

"Yes, it is. Mia needed help with the paint and I couldn't resist helping her." I smiled, tilting my head and matched Eden's glare. "I always loved playing with colors."

Sensing the tension brimming between the two of us, Mia cleared her throat and packed up her bag, clutching the sketchbook to her chest. "I'll see you later."

"*Wait.*" I stood up and slid the lunch I had prepared for her that morning. Even though she was mad, I didn't want her to miss a meal. "Your lunch."

Mia's cheeks flushed red as she took the Tupperware and murmured a quick, 'Thank you' before rushing out of the room.

As much as I wanted to keep her with me in a locked room, the art classroom wasn't the best place. Especially when it was a school, and it was forbidden to have any sort of teacher-student relationship.

"You seem close to the Miller girl," the dean noted.

I shrugged, sliding my hands in my pockets, thankful that one look from her had made my boner wilt away. "I told you before, she's Clyde's daughter."

I had chosen to teach during Mia's year for a specific reason, to look after her. Especially when she was hell bent on trying to get admission in Saint Helena Academy because her mother wanted the best for her daughter.

"What did you want to talk about?" I asked, knowing full well where the conversation was going.

"I know you're living together, James." Her voice was soft, but her tone wasn't. "You'd be in a serious position if something happened between the two of you."

"Is that so?" I hummed and walked around the desk, closing the distance between us until I whispered in her ear, "If I were you, Eden, I'd invest in a gag ball." I pulled away when she gasped at me. "You're pretty loud when one of your students fucks you in your office after school."

"Y-you..." she sputtered, her cheeks turning into an angry shade of red.

"I teach an art class, Eden. Not to mention, I am the owner of a billion dollar company, so you should have put a little more thought into who you're threatening." I checked my watch. "I'll catch you later, dean. Oh, don't forget to get the silicone one. I've heard they can be used for a longer time."

Smirking at her scowled-flushed face, I walked out of the classroom and exhaled the breath I was holding. If I didn't have the upper hand with her, things could have gone drastically wrong.

My classes for the day were over and I had a few designs to look through, so I locked myself in my office in the other building. I could drive to Fox Constructs, but I wasn't in the mood to talk to my employees or face my personal assistant just yet. I wanted to wait for Mia so I could drive us home together and maybe even get pizza on the way if she wanted.

Before I knew it, the school was over and there was a sharp knock on my office door.

"Enter," I said, not bothering to look up from my laptop. I knew who it was just by the cherry scent of her perfume.

"Are you busy?" Her voice was small, and she seemed nervous.

Looking up from the screen, I found Mia was nibbling on

her bottom lip and fidgeting with her fingers. Removing my glasses, I pulled my chair back and patted my thigh.

"Come here, Princess."

Her legs moved, and I welcomed her warm body onto my lap, seating her comfortably on my thighs. I raked my fingers through her hair, feeling much more relaxed than before as her cherry scent engulfed me.

"Why are you nervous?" I asked, tilting her chin to look at me.

Her tongue peeked out to wet her lips and my hand tightened on her thigh. "You don't regret it, right?"

Regret?

I frowned and pulled her closer, cupping her cheek. "If you're talking about kissing you, no, Mia, I don't fucking regret kissing you, even though I should. Do you regret it?"

I stayed still, and I wasn't sure if I was even breathing to hear her answer.

Shaking her head, she wrapped her arms around me. "I don't. I-I want to do more than kiss you, James."

Thank fuck.

"Yeah?" I smiled and claimed her lips in a soft kiss. Keeping my forehead on hers, I took a deep breath and said, "If you ever want to stop this… whatever this is, just say the word and I won't bother you again, Princess. I promise. I… I don't want to hurt you. Intentionally or not."

Mia must have seen how sincere I was and cupped my cheeks. "I don't want to stop. I trust you." She smiled and added, "You can never hurt me, James, unless it's spankings."

I chuckled and squeezed her butt, knowing the skin was healing well and it wasn't sore anymore. "Spankings are a fun way to punish and discipline naughty brats like you, Princess. And you love them, so shush." I kissed her nose and said, "Let's get out of here. I've something to show you."

Her eyes twinkled. "What is it?"
"It's a surprise, Princess."
"Another sex toy shop?"
"You'll have to see it for yourself."

23
IT'S A GIFT

MIA

"No." I shook my head, staring at it and again shaking my head. "No. No way. No. No way."

"I heard you the first time." James seemed unaffected when he walked towards it, dragging me behind him. His hand pressed the key fob in my palm and I felt dread creeping up my spine and spreading all over my body.

"I... I can't," I whispered, thinking back to the smell of medicine and blood in that cold hospital room. "You can't do this."

His blue orbs flickered to my face, and I forgot how to breathe for a moment. He seemed younger in casual clothing, with his hair damp from the shower. Apparently, the surprise he wanted to show me was at my place, but I needed to clean up before he showed it to me. I was expecting two tickets for a movie or a concert, but instead, he gave me car keys.

Yes. I was joking about him being my Sugar Daddy, but I didn't know my subconscious was so powerful that it manifested into reality. Or maybe it was because of my subliminal phase back when I was thirteen and really wanted a Sugar

Daddy buying me everything I wanted and kept listening to it for hours.

Oh God, no, I take it all back.

"I already did, Princess." He nodded at the car which was sleek black because he didn't know which pastel color I'd like. He can get it repainted if I change my mind. *Yes, James Fox is clinically insane.* "Get in the car."

"No." I stayed rooted at my spot on the side road and looked around, wishing someone would save me. "You can't give someone a car for a surprise."

"I just did." He blinked at me and leaned back on the car. Fuck him and his long legs and those fucking dark locks that made him look like a hot edge lord. An edge lord I wanted to fuck.

"Well... take it back."

"Gifts are not supposed to be returned, Mia."

"I don't want it," I snapped and closed my eyes. Taking a deep breath, I answered, "I don't want a car from you."

His eyes darkened. "Why not?"

"Because... because I wanted to buy it for myself." I threw my hands in the air. "Cars are expensive and I can't take this from you—"

James straightened up and took a step closer, looming over me with his height. "Listen to me, Princess, and don't make me repeat myself. You're not taking anything from me. I'm giving it to you. Your birthday present, and it's a gift. For you and for my peace of mind."

"Your peace of mind?"

"Yes," he said, and opened the driver's door. Thankfully, it wasn't an electric car like his or else I'd have fainted. But it was still expensive enough to make me feel lightheaded. "Get in the car."

"Is everything okay?"

James' jaw twitched again as we both turned to see Aiden Stone, the hot therapist next door who was whipped by the sweet Ivy. I had suspected they were in a relationship and whooped the loudest when Ivy invited me, Dad and even James to their engagement party. I was in awe because Ivy's brother, Hayden, became the Prince of Azmia after marrying the Princess of Azmia. I could proudly add in my resume that I've met all the royals of Azmia and ate *kunafah* with them.

"No, it's not," I answered before James could and his face snapped to me, his eyes flashing and a vein popping on his neck. If I wasn't so nervous, I'd have licked it. "James is forcefully giving me this car."

I was relieved when Ivy walked over, her innocent face darting between me and James, and accepting me with open arms. They both had given us a visit after hearing about Dad's health and offered me a huge casserole and lots of ice cream.

"Forcefully giving you a car?" Ivy asked.

James crossed his arms and glared at me. "It's a gift. She's turning eighteen a day after tomorrow and it's her birthday gift."

Aiden nodded as if understanding what I was going through, but then said, "Oh, it's a gift. Then it's alright."

"No, it's not," Ivy and I said in unison. We both shared a smile before turning towards the men.

"A car is too much for a gift," Ivy said, and I exclaimed, 'Exactly!' which earned me another glare from James. I bet he was counting how many spanks I was going to get once we get home but I didn't care. Spanking was fun, but I was going to stand my ground.

"Petal, I bought you a house," Aiden said with a soft voice to his fiancée. I mentally cooed at the sweet nickname he had for her. "Car is nothing, especially for a birthday gift."

James narrowed his eyes at the other man and cleared his throat. "Exactly. Car is nothing, Princess. I can get you a house if you want. Anything you want."

How about bouncing me on that thick dick—

Not. Now.

Flushing with embarrassment and my dirty thoughts, I said, "I don't want a car. I wanted to buy it with my own money and…"

He shrugged. "Buy it with yours whenever you want, Mia. I'm not stopping you. I don't want you to depend on me or Clyde or your friends whenever you need a ride. I'm gifting you your freedom." He looked away, a red blush creeping up his neck and ears. "But if you really don't want it, then I'll get you something else."

"Aww." Ivy cupped her mouth and cleared her throat. "I mean, James is right, Mia."

"You too?" I stared at her accusingly.

Aiden gave both of us a knowing smile and wrapped his arm around Ivy's waist. "I think you have to figure this out on your own and talk out your limits for gifts with James." *Thank you, feelings doctor.* "I've a present I've to give Petal, so if you'll excuse us."

I winked at Ivy because we all knew what 'present' Aiden was talking about. The man couldn't keep his hands to himself when she was around, and I was glad that both of our houses had thick walls.

"Come here."

My heartbeat doubled hearing *that* tone, and I moved towards him. His eyes were dark and under the moonlight, his sharp face looked like it belonged to a painting.

"Drive the car, Princess," he whispered, cupping my cheek and brushing his thumb over my lips. Lifting his eyes from them, he added, "If you don't accept this present, I've tons of other gift ideas."

I took a step closer and wrapped my arms around him, peering up at his handsome face. "Why don't you give me the one thing I want?"

"My penis?"

"Something like that." I rolled my eyes at his grin, blushing at the sight. I loved it when he grinned or laughed. It made his eyes soften and my heart felt mushy.

Leaning down, he kissed my forehead. "Soon, Princess."

"Come now," he pulled away and pulled me towards the driver's seat. "Go take this baby for a ride."

I sat down on the seat and watched him walk over to the passenger seat and buckle in. Taking a deep breath, I turned on the engine of the car and grinned at the smooth purr.

"I've a license, just so you know," I said and slowly shifted the gear before turning around and focusing on the road.

"I know that, Princess." I felt his eyes on the side of my face, but I didn't want to look at him. If I did, I would crash because I wouldn't be able to look away. "You can drive a little faster, you know?"

"I…" I swallowed the lump in my throat and tightened my hold on the wheel. "I'm scared."

He didn't reply for a few moments. "Scared of what?"

"That I'll crash." I blinked quickly and my heart tightened just at the thought of it. "And you'll get hurt."

A warm hand landed on my thigh and I relaxed a little when his deep voice said, "You won't crash, Princess. I'm here."

I nodded and shuffled on the seat. "Distract me."

I glanced towards him in time to see his delicious smirk and shook my head when his hand inched closer to the hem of my shorts.

"N-no, James." I bit my lip and clenched my legs together. "Not that type of distraction unless you really want me to crash."

"Then what type of distraction, Princess?" He was practically purring, caressing my inner thigh as if he couldn't wait to dive his hand inside my underwear.

"Tell me about your Mom."

24
I'LL SPANK YOU

MIA

When his hand froze on my thigh, I looked over at him and quickly added, "Or not. Forget it. I was thinking about my Mom and figured I should—"

"Mia. It's okay." He took away the hand from my lap, and, despite aching for his touch, I let him continue. "She was pretty clever. I could never have the last word with her when we argued. And she was a nuisance."

"Such a big nuisance." He was smiling sadly when he continued, "Always laughing and pranking me. She was a kid in an adult's body with wisdom beyond her age. We'd be laughing one moment, and the next second she'd tell me some shit about life and how I should help others before pranking me with a fake bug."

I looked away and kept my eyes on the road, swerving and using the auto gear. "She seems lovely."

"She was."

Was. *Again*.

Swallowing the lump in my throat, I asked, "What happened?"

He knew what I was talking about. He must have heard from Dad how my mom passed away in—

"She died in a car accident."

I took a sharp breath and momentarily lost my grip on the steering wheel. I stole a quick glance and found him glaring out of the window, his hand clenched in a fist on his lap. With as much gentleness as I could muster, I placed my hand over his. I exhaled the breath I was holding when he entwined our hands together, his thumb stroking patterns on my knuckles.

"I'm sorry," I said when we reached the hospital, parking the car perfectly on the spot.

"It's okay, Princess." James met my eyes and smiled. It didn't reach his eyes, but still he leaned closer and kissed my forehead. "Let's go meet Clyde before he harasses his nurse about Star Wars again."

I nodded and held back a few questions. I wanted to know how the accident happened. Why and how did it happen? But James wasn't used to opening up and telling me about his mom and how she... it was a big deal. I would respect his decision and wait for him to share anything he wanted to on his own terms.

Wow, look at me. I almost sound like an adult in my head.

Soon. I will be an adult soon.

* * *

"ARE WE SERIOUSLY WATCHING *TANGLED* AGAIN?" James groaned, hearing my evil little giggle. "Let's try something—"

"No."

"*Mia.*"

"I want to see Flynn Ryder. It's my birthday."

"It's not your birthday until the clock strikes twelve, you

little brat." I ignored him and settled on the couch. "We literally watched Tangled with Clyde yesterday!"

I deadpanned, "And your point?"

He glared at me. "I'll spank you."

I smirked and let out a very high-pitched moan, "Spank me, Daddy! Oh, yes—*James!* Oops—Daddy yes, yes spank me—*ow!*"

Giggles and laughter kept bubbling out of me when he pinned me on the couch, tickling me and turning me around to land a playful spank on my butt. I wriggled at him and looked over my shoulder to find him grinning down at me.

With a sparkling idea, I wriggled out of his hold and ran upstairs. Finding everything I needed, I trudged down, sighing when he took the blankets from my hand and asked me,

"Do you plan to sleep in the living room?"

"No, silly." I grinned. "We are making a blanket fort!"

He raised his brows and watched me struggle with the pile of blankets. His sigh echoed through the living room before he came to help me. It took a few minutes and a lot of struggle from my side because my arms were like noodles while his were made of muscles and tears of students.

James even surprised me by bringing a few stuffed toys from my collection and settled beside me when I started the movie. I had a bunch of candle jars Summer had given me when she was in her candle-making phase, so I lit them up, placing them carefully around the fort. I was laughing and holding the elephant stuffed toy he had gifted me when he leaned closer to take a sip from my mug of hot chocolate.

"It's mine!" I gasped but let the thief taste delicious heaven.

He lifted a brow, licking his lips. "I made it for you."

"So? I was there to give you emotional support when you made it and poured all my—"

"*Shh.*" He placed his finger on my lips and leaned closer. My lids fluttered when his face was inches away from me. I waited impatiently for him to capture my lips in his, but when he moved closer, he took another sip from the mug.

"You're a thief!" I pouted, pulling away and chugging the entire mug of hot chocolate.

"You're such a brat," he said, shaking his head and smiling at me.

"Says the man who stole two sips of my hot chocolate—w-what are you doing?" I asked in a low voice when he kept the empty mug away and crowded my personal space. I tried to move back, but we were in a blanket fort and there were stacks of pillows behind me.

I closed my eyes when his face neared and his tongue licked my lips. Shivers of pleasure rolled through my body and I parted my lips to kiss him. His hand swept through my hair as he angled my face closer and kissed me. I moaned when he bit my bottom lip before licking it better and diving in to taste me.

My chest arched towards him as his other hand slipped inside my nightshirt. His hand was cold, but it felt so good against my skin. I pulled him closer, spreading my legs so he could settle between my thighs and I could tug at his tee shirt.

"Easy, Princess." He grinned, pulling away and tucking a lock of hair behind my ear. "Don't you want to finish the movie?"

I couldn't believe I was doing it, but I shook my head. "Kiss me, Daddy."

"Anything you want, Princess." He closed his lips around me once more, pressing my back on the mattress we had placed underneath. I gasped when I felt his hard length brush against my center and how violently I ached for his touch. For *more*.

His lips moved on my neck, and I had to scrunch my fingers on the sheets to hold on to something. I arched and squirmed, moaning his name when his lips lowered to my shirt. I gasped when he tore it open, the buttons flying away.

"You tore my shirt—*oh*, d-don't stop." My fingers feathered his hair when his hot mouth sucked on my nipple. His hand squeezed and kneaded my other breast, licking, biting, and pinching my nipples with his hands and teeth.

"Fucking love your tits, Princess," he whispered, pulling away to repeat his actions on the other side. "I'm going to make them prettier with hickeys, okay?"

I nodded, but I didn't think he was asking me. He was telling me that he was marking my breasts—*tits*, as he calls them, with hickeys. My teeth pressed into my bottom lip when he bit my skin, his teeth and lips sucking the sensitive tip of my nipple and pulling away before giving it a soft kiss.

My eyes were half-lidded and watching his every move when he leaned back on his heels to tug off his tee shirt. I licked my lips, gazing at his muscles. He wasn't bulky with muscles, but his broad shoulders, tapered waist and abs made my mouth water. My eyes drifted to the large bulge in his pants, but before I could move to touch him, James was upon me.

"I'm going to teach my Princess how to cum."

25

BLANKET FORT

MIA

"Yes, please, Daddy," I breathed out, squirming with anticipation and need.

He hummed against my belly, kissing and caressing every inch of my skin before slipping down my shorts. He groaned, spreading my legs wide, his finger pressing against my clit through the underwear.

"So fucking wet. Did you soak your panties for Daddy, hm, Princess?" he asked, his voice rough and eyes full of lust.

"I-I did," I moaned when his hand rubbed over my sensitive bundle of nerves. "P-please make me cum, Daddy."

"Such a good fucking girl," he whispered, his eyes glazed. "You are bare, Princess. Did you shave for me?"

My cheeks flushed, and I gave him a shy nod. "I-I got a Brazilian for tomorrow's pool party." *With Emma and Summer.* It was my first time getting it as I was used to trimming or shaving, but it felt really good and ticklish to get it waxed.

His grip tightened on my thigh. "Next time, I'll do it for you."

"What?" I squeaked. *Next time?*

"I'll shave your pretty little cunt. I don't want anyone else seeing my pussy." His eyes were on his fingers that were moving over my thong and providing me enough friction that I was already on the edge.

"Please make me cum."

"I will, Princess." James groaned, "I will. Let me taste you. Just once—"

I cried out when his mouth lowered between my legs. He didn't even wait to remove my panties, no he slid it to the side and planted his mouth on my pussy. I squeezed my eyes shut at the toe-curling sensation. His tongue licking my slicked lips before moving to my clit.

"Your taste—*fuck*, Princess." His blue eyes flickered to me and I gasped when he tore off my panties. "I'll teach you later, for now, I want to eat you out. Taste your pretty little pussy."

"James—*ohohoh!*" I tried to move my hips when his mouth landed on my heated center, his tongue licking my clit while his lips sucked on it. I was going to cum. I could feel it.

"Moan for me, pretty Princess," he grunted, the reverberations of his voice sending shivers down my spine. "Moan for Daddy, my pretty little slut."

I obeyed him. Moaning and gasping when his mouth licked me all over. I felt like a strung up instrument he was strumming for his own pleasure.

"More, please!" I begged, whimpering, when he inserted a finger inside me, his eyes on my face to note every expression.

"That hurt?" he asked, his face inches away from my pussy. When I shook my head, he slowly slid another finger inside me. My walls clamped around him and I gasped at the stretch and weird sensation of being full. "Fucking hell, Mia. You're tight as fuck."

"James..." I felt so embarrassed, but the things he was doing to me were so lewd. "I... I feel like I'll pee."

"You won't, Princess." He grinned at me and slowly started moving his fingers inside me. "You're about to cum, baby. Let me see you orgasm."

His tongue peeked out, and I whimpered when he licked my clit. "Let it go, Princess. Focus on me and cum on my mouth." He groaned and spread my thighs wider, flashing his dark blue eyes at me. "Cum on your Daddy's tongue."

That did it. I squeezed my eyes shut when he curled his fingers inside me, hitting the sensitive spot that made me see stars. I moaned, groaned and whimpered through the immense release of the pleasure, my legs trembling as pleasure after pleasure rolled through me in waves.

"Happy Birthday, Princess," James whispered and dove in once again.

"Thank you, Daddy—*ah*," I moaned again, feeling his lips and tongue on my pussy. Licking me up. "I..."

"*Shh*," he said, tightening his hold on my thighs and stopping me from snapping them shut, "Let me clean you up."

I bit my lip and shivered, blinking my eyes through the blurred vision and looked up at the blankets that covered us. *Oh my God*. James kissed me and ate me out in a blanket fort.

"S-stop," I whimpered, feeling the overstimulation when his tongue played with the swollen nub. "I'm sensitive."

His eyes drifted to my face, and he finally pulled back, licking his lips and raking his gaze through my naked body as if I was his prey.

"You're lucky it was your first time or else I'd have loved to have you overstimulated and keep you cumming for me." I bit my lip, feeling lightheaded when he hovered above me, his thumb brushing my bottom lip and teasing it out. "How'd you feel, Princess?"

"Good." I licked my lips and added, "I feel like I'm floating."

He chuckled and leaned down to kiss me. I moaned, tasting my musky scent on his lips and tongue. We were both panting when we pulled away, his cheeks flushed and eyes clear.

"Sorry, I got carried away." He pulled me over his chest, his hand running through my hair. "I wanted to teach you, but I had to eat you out."

My cheeks flushed, and I snuggled closer to him, wrapping my arms around him. "It's okay. I enjoyed it a lot, Daddy."

"I could see and hear that, Princess," he whispered in my ear. "I knew you were a screamer."

I noticed the tent in his pants and peered at him. "You're hard."

"Why wouldn't I be after eating out the prettiest girl?"

"I… I want to make you cum, too."

"Don't worry about it." He stopped my hand from drifting lower. "Go to sleep or let me eat you out again."

I frowned, but I was feeling sleepy after experiencing my very first orgasm. Yawning, I let my eyes drift shut and listened to his calming heartbeat.

* * *

"Why did you have to give me hickies?" I whined, applying more water-proof concealer on my breasts, which I never thought I would do.

James was sprawled on my queen size bed and somehow, he dwarfed it with his size as he hummed, picking up my bikini bottoms.

"You weren't complaining when my mouth was on your breast."

"James!"

"I can make you scream louder than that, Princess." He leaned up, supporting his head in his hand, and smirked at me. "Wanna try?"

I scowled and crossed my arms, turning around and facing him. Which was a mistake because I wasn't wearing anything on the top and his eyes dropped to my breasts.

"I promised Emma that I'll reach her house by eleven." I continued applying the setting powder on my breasts. "It's one in the afternoon now."

He shrugged and stood up from the bed. "Not my fault someone was passed out in their blanket fort and won't wake up when I asked them to."

"It *is* your fault," I pointed out with flushed cheeks, remembering the night before.

"Oh, yeah?" He stepped closer, wrapping his arms around me and sliding his hand underneath my shorts. "Do you want a repeat of last night, Princess? Or should I make you grind your cunt on my fingers for being such a brat, hm?"

26
COWARD
JAMES

Before I could slide my fingers to feel her wet heat, we were interrupted by the ringtone of her phone. Her phone screen flashed with her friend's name and a sweet picture of them together in a selfie.

Keeping my mouth beside her ear, I whispered, "Tell her you'll be late." My fingers lowered to her clit, groaning to find it hard and swollen. "I need to eat you out again."

"James—*mm!*" she whimpered when I landed a light spank on her clit and she corrected, "Daddy, please."

"Please what, Princess?" I licked the soft arch of her neck, tasting her skin and humming in approval when she moved her hips, pressing her clit on my fingers for friction. "Come now, don't make me repeat myself."

Mia answered the phone. Her voice was shaky when she said, "Hey, Em. Yes." Pause. Her bright green eyes met mine from the reflection of the mirror as I kissed her neck, resisting the urge to give her a hickey. "Uhhhh, I'm s-sorry. I'll be a little late."

I grabbed her breast, slowly squeezing it and pinching the pebbled nipple. Her hips jerked, and she pressed back at me, her ass grinding against my bulge, making me groan. I moved my digits faster and slid them lower to find her pussy drenched. Sinking my finger inside her was easy, and the tight feeling of her walls made me grind against her little ass harder.

"Daddy," she moaned and my eyes flashed in her mirror. I hadn't even realized she had hung up the phone. Her fingers clenching my forearms as I kept fucking her pussy with my fingers. I pinched her nipple harder and buried my face in her neck, inhaling her sweet cherry scent.

I wanted to throw her on her queen size bed with a floral blanket and fuck her like my little princess slut.

"Your cunt is so fucking tight, Princess," I grunted, curling my fingers inside her. "Makes me think you're a virgin."

I opened my eyes when she took a sharp intake of breath. Mia's eyes were wide, and she was no longer holding onto my arms. She swallowed, making her throat bob.

What the fuck?

I pulled away and took a step back. "Don't tell me that you…" I turned away, willing my dick to turn soft, but that new information was both scary yet sexy. Raking my hand through my hair, I paced around her room. "You're a virgin. *Fuck.*"

She straightened her shorts and wore her bikini, covering her breasts that had hickeys all over them. *Fuck me.* I was the one who had marked her with them and had my mouth on her pussy. My mouth watered just at the thought of her sweet taste.

"Why does it matter?" Mia asked, scowling at me. "I told you I have never orgasmed before."

"I thought he didn't make you cum when you fucked." I laughed sinfully. "How are you even a virgin? You used to go on dates and—"

"I didn't want to have sex," she whispered and looked

away from me. "I wasn't ready, but now I am and you're acting weird."

Tension thickened in her room and I couldn't stand staring at her. She looked so sweet and innocent in the cute white top with denim shorts, her hair piled up high in a ponytail with a few wisps of hair framing her dainty face. Clenching my jaw, I looked away. I couldn't do it. Not when she was a virgin.

"Forget about it, Mia," I said, my voice firm even when her eyes gleamed with tears. My heart hurt, but I had to do it. "I can't—"

She chuckled, and it was humorless, raising the hair on my arms. "You're such a fucking coward." My brows raised when she stabbed her finger on my chest. "*Coward*. Me being a virgin doesn't change anything. It's a fucking social construct. I've been asking you to have sex with me and I know you want the same."

"Princess, you shouldn't have your first time with your teacher, your dad's best friend, who is twice your fucking age," I grit out, clenching my hands to stop myself from holding her. "I can't do it."

"Oh, so now you want to act all high and mighty by bringing the age in." She was seething, her face red with anger. "Fuck you."

"*Princess...*"

"Don't call me that." Picking up her purse and the key fob of her new car, she turned towards me. "If you don't want to fuck me, then I'll just find someone else."

I glared at her when she walked out of the room. My vision burned just thinking about her touching someone else other than me. The thought of Mia showing off her sweet smile and daring anyone else to hear her moans made me see red.

Like hell I'd let her.

Mia

Slamming the car door a little too harshly, I stomped my way across Emma's porch and forced a smile on one of the servants, who opened the main doors. How dare he. I hate him. At one moment he was all over me, whispering filthy things in my ear, and then cold as ice, trying to be honorable.

Emma's driveway was filled with cars. Her main hall was covered with party decorations. Streamers taped to the walls and dangling from lights, 'Mia's Birthday!' balloons hanging from the ceiling. Talking and laughter shrieked through the backyard where the pool was and the delicious smell of burgers wafted into the house. I couldn't wait to go outside and show off my bikini, and make some wrong choices on my birthday.

So what if James didn't want to sleep with me. I had plenty of other options. Or at least I hoped I had.

Caterers were moving through the hall, and I wondered why the heck Emma needed to spend so much on just a birthday. I appreciated the thought, but it felt extravagant. I made my way upstairs, towards the east wing where Emma's room was and Summer pounced on me as soon as I entered the suite that was Em's room.

"Happy birthday, my bestest friend in the entire world —*oh*. I think you need this more than I do." Summer's wide grin softened into a confused smile then in awe when I accepted the red cup and swallowed the burning drink in one go. It tasted like shit, but at least it matched my mood.

"You okay?" Emma asked, standing up from the dresser, her blond curls hanging perfectly over her shoulder. Her makeup was flawless, and she wore a lilac pink see through robe over her hot pink bikini. "You need one more cup of that... *thing*."

I nodded, glancing at Summer, who was donning a white

two-piece bikini that matched her golden-brown skin. She looked like an absolute goddess with her curls brushing her shoulder.

"Can you make me something strong? I really need it." I sat down on the empty stool and met Emma's eyes in the mirror. "Emma, I need to look more sexy. More... I don't know. I don't want to look like this for sure."

"Babe, you are sexy." She glanced at Summer, who was making some pink drink that looked scary. "But it's your birthday. We'll do whatever you want."

Anything you want, Princess. I'll do anything you want.

Anything *but* fuck me. I clenched my hands in my lap and nodded. "Yes. I want to look sexy, get drunk and have fun. Without any men."

"Not even Caleb?" Emma asked, patting something on my face that smelt like strawberries. Summer handed me another drink.

"Caleb is fine," I said and took a big sip of the sweet but burning liquid. It tasted like cherries, but had a weird aftertaste to it. My head was feeling well-buzzed after one cup, and although Emma scolded me for having another drink, Summer gave me a can of beer.

"You look like a doll!"

True to their words, they had changed up my appearance with the magic of makeup and curling iron. My green eyes were lined with kohl and the smoky makeup made them look brighter. I had dabbed blush on my cheeks and applied plum red lipstick that made my lips full. With dark soft waves brushing my back, I looked ready for war.

Both of them cooed when I stood up from the stool feeling well cared for. I could always count on them for cheering me.

Emma handed me a gloss while Summer whistled,

looking at me. "You should be thankful we haven't hired any strippers like last time."

My face flamed thinking about Summer's eighteenth birthday party. "I'm ready." I took a deep breath and smiled at both of them. "Let's get this party started!"

27
TRUTH OR DARE?

MIA

"Chug, chug, chug!" Everyone chanted as I kept swallowing the beer, my hand clenching on the can when I pulled away, laughing with the crowd of tipsy classmates. Others were already swimming in the pool, lounging on the chair aka making out under the shade, or playing ping-pong, or truth or dare.

Not to mention the constant supply of alcohol and burgers. Emma sure knew how to host a party.

"I never knew you had it in you, Mia," Aaron chuckled, leaning closer. "Ditch the clothes. Everyone is already half-naked."

Looking around, most of them were flaunting their bodies in shorts, bikinis or swimming trunks. Aaron tugged off his shirt, flaunting his muscled body, grinning at me.

"Come on, birthday girl."

"Fine, fine," I muttered, biting my lip and crossing my arms. Before I could remove the loose top I was wearing, I looked across the backyard towards the open glass doors where James was standing.

I knew he was invited, but I didn't think he would actually come to a silly birthday party after fighting with me.

I couldn't make out his face from the distance so I didn't know what he was thinking, but I could feel his burning gaze on me.

Fuck him. I removed my top and unzipped my denim shorts to let them pool around my ankles. I shivered, more so because of the feeling of being watched than the breeze caressing my bare skin.

Aaron let out a wolf whistle, making my face feel hot. Holding my hand, he dragged me to the pool. He didn't wait for an answer before lifting me in his arms and diving into the cool water. I let out a squeal and clutched him when I was swallowed by the cold, coming up for air and angrily splashing water on his laughing face. *Thank god the makeup was waterproof.*

The burn on my neck returned, but I ignored it. *What if James was right? What if I should be with a guy my age?* Maybe someone like Aaron, and, with time, the silly crush on James might disappear.

It wouldn't hurt to try, *would it?*

* * *

I DON'T KNOW how much time had passed except that the sun had already set and everyone around me was drunk and happy. Emma's mom, Dorothy, had called her once without giving us any attention. We were used to her mother being cold, and I was relieved to see Em smiling when she came back, which was a rare sight after talking to her mother.

"Come on, truth or dare!" Most of us were in the pool and instead of playing the usual truth or dare, we were taking turns and I was excited because it was my turn next.

"Truth."

I snorted when Claire chose the truth, and gulped down the drink in my hand. I wasn't completely shit faced yet, but I was very, very tipsy with my body swaying as the cold water lapped at my body lazily. I felt like jumping off the cliff or going to hibernate. Or skinny dip.

I giggled to myself, ignoring Claire glaring at me.

"If you could fuck someone from our faculty, who would it be and why?"

I scoffed at the silly question one guy asked. Of course, they'd ask the most boring and horny question.

"James, of course." Claire answered, flicking her hair over her shoulder and my grip tightened on the cup, hating the images that flashed in my head of James and her together. Touching her like he touched me. Getting naked with her. Fucking her. I hated myself for getting jealous. "He's the hottest and don't tell me you wouldn't fuck him if you had the chance."

Most of the girls and even guys agreed, joking about him which infuriated me further. I looked away, wishing I could get out of the pool and maybe eat something—

"Truth or dare, birthday girl."

My neck prickled at everyone's attention on me. I knew what they wanted me to choose. So I drowned the content of alcohol from the cup and licked my lips.

"Dare."

Guys whooped and discussed their worst dare. My stomach clenched and found the concerned stare of Emma and Summer. They were standing across from me and had already completed their truth and dares. Summer chose dare and had to take body shots from a girl's stomach. Em chose truth and told us about the time she skinny dipped in her farmhouse in Italy while her boyfriend, Caleb, chose dare, locking him and a girl from cheer team in a closet for seven minutes in heaven. I was surprised that Emma didn't react without so much as an arch of brow while her boyfriend couldn't stop blushing.

"How about you come with me, Mia?"

My eyes widened seeing the flush on Aaron's cheeks when he asked me the question. Everyone was subtly staring at both of us, and I knew if I said no, they'd groan and give me something else to do like body shots or bring them more beer. I didn't want to do either of them.

And I wanted to *try*. Even though my stomach tightened with the thought, I agreed, ignoring the way my classmates snickered when I held Aaron's hand before getting out of the pool. I even ignored the remark of someone shouting, "Wrap it before you tap it, Aaron!" and dried my body with a towel before shuffling on my shorts.

I swallowed the lump in my throat when he locked the door behind us after entering one of the many guest rooms. Aaron stood across from me and I could see the hesitation in his light brown eyes. The small tremble in his hand. James never hesitated before doing whatever he wanted. His hand didn't shake when—

Why the hell am I comparing Aaron to him?

"Aaron, I don't know why you asked me for this dare."

He looked surprised and chuckled lightly, running a hand through his golden hair. God, he was really cute, but... my stupid heart and body liked someone else.

"I didn't think you'd be so oblivious, Mia."

"Oblivious?" I didn't understand what he meant.

Aaron looked at me and said, "I like you, Mia. Since the first day of school, I made up excuses to be around you."

My cheeks heated and all of a sudden, I felt vulnerable and too open in front of him because I never noticed it.

"But you paid me for all your homework and—"

"I did it to spend time with you, Mia," he said, without a beat. "I know, it's pathetic but I didn't know how to approach you or ask you out so when I came to know about it, I asked you."

I was stunned. I didn't expect him to say that to me. I didn't know what I expected, but it wasn't... *this*.

"I want to kiss you," he said, but didn't lean towards me. "But I know you don't like me."

"Aaron... I'm—"

He narrowed his eyes at me. "Don't you dare say sorry or apologize for my crush. I just wanted to tell you about my feelings, and if you feel the same way..." He shrugged, sliding his hands in his pockets, "Maybe we can be in a relationship."

"I don't," I said too quickly. "I mean. I don't like you in a romantic way."

I couldn't meet his eyes when the awkward silence stretched between us. But I was relieved that nothing would happen between us. Relieved *yet* disappointed.

"Maybe I should go..." I trailed off, waiting for him to say something, but his face looked like a puppy who had just been kicked, and I didn't know what else to do.

Should I hug him? Pet his head?

"Yeah. I'll see you in school," he said and before I could open the door, he added, "Sorry about the care. My friends wanted us to get alone so I could man up, but... *yeah*."

"It's okay, Aaron." I flashed him a small smile. "I'm glad we had this talk."

I didn't wait for his reply and walked away. My head ran with so many thoughts, I didn't even notice where I was going.

Aaron liked me. More than friends and—

Before I could scream, someone clamped their hand on my mouth and dragged me out of the silent hallway. Dread filled me when I heard the sharp snip of a door being locked.

What the fuck.

28
YOU'RE BIG

MIA

I tried to wriggle away, but they tightened their hold on my waist and panic settled in my brain until he neared enough for me to recognize his touch. His powerful arms and his scent. Pine and soft musk.

"Did he fuck you good, Princess?" James grumbled, the hair on my arms raising at his low tone. He moved, pinning me to the wall with his hips pressed tight against my ass. "*Hm?* Did he, sweet girl?"

I shivered hearing him coo those words in my ear, his large hands gliding over my stomach to my breasts and wrapping around my neck. I whimpered, squeezing my eyes shut.

"W-What are you doing, James?"

"*Tsk.*" He pushed deeper, making me moan, and covered my mouth with his hand that was on my neck. "Did he make you moan like that when he fucked you?" His words turned into a rough growl that had me squirming against him. "*Hm*, my little birthday slut?"

His other hand undid the button and zipper on my shorts, shoving his hand in my panties and rubbing my clit. James chuckled, his sound deep. "Look at you. Your pussy is soaked, Mia."

I tried to say something, but his hand was muffling my words. In an instant, he turned me around, pinning my back to the wall. My eyes widened, trying to see him through the darkness, but the only light flittered in through the open windows. His dark silhouette loomed over me, pressing against me again, his hand still in my underwear.

"I can't hear you, Princess," he mocked, tilting his head.

It was so embarrassing and humiliating. Letting him cover my mouth and rub my clit like that in total darkness while he taunted me. Yet I was so, so turned on, my panties getting wetter by each second.

A moan escaped my lips and my hips moved over his hand, trying to grind against his deft fingers and gain more friction. I yelped through his hand when I felt the sharp sting on my thigh, his hand no longer on my pussy.

I took a sharp breath when his face moved closer, his minty breath caressing my cheek. "I'm going to move my hand, Princess, so don't utter a word unless I tell you to. Understood?"

I nodded, eyes wide. Alcohol still buzzed through me and it was my birthday. I wasn't going to do shit unless I wanted to. Not because someone, especially him, asked me to.

As soon as he pulled away his hand, I grabbed his collar and kissed him. He must have been shocked because I was biting his bottom lip and tugging at his hair. It was rough, angry, and passionate. I wanted to show him how much I hated him, yet wanted him. I moaned when he kissed me back, holding the back of my neck and slipping his tongue inside me—

"Mia," he murmured, moving away, breaking the kiss. "*Stop.*"

"No, I don't want to." I tried to kiss him again, but he

stopped me, glaring at me. I could make out his piercing eyes in the dark and his heaving chest and... *oh*.

He was hard.

"Why not?"

"Because you're drunk."

I chuckled and moved my hair over my shoulder. "If I was drunk, I'd have passed out by now. Let me kiss you, James."

When he didn't reply or even look at me, I took a step towards him, dropping my voice into a low whisper and trailing my fingers over the dark shirt he wore.

"Let me kiss you, Daddy."

By the sharp intake of breath, I knew I had him. But I wanted more. It was *my* birthday. Removing all the space between us, I tipped on my toes and kissed his neck, humming and licking it before sucking on his hot skin. The sighs he made were so erotic that I was scratching on his shirt like a needy kitten.

Pulling away, I dropped my knees on the floor and licking my lips. I stared at the bulge in his pants.

"Fuck, Mia," he grumbled and held my hand before I could touch him. "You don't have to—"

"I want to." I tried to meet his eyes and said with a soft but firm voice, "Let me. *Please, Daddy.*"

Even I knew he wouldn't be able to deny such a sweet request from me. I smirked in victory when he pulled his hand away. I hoped he didn't notice how my hands were shaking when I unbuckled his belt, or how I was swallowing thickly because he seemed huge.

"Oh, God..." I muttered, blinking at the outline of his dick in his boxers. I leaned up and licked him through the fabric, flickering my eyes at his face that was hidden in the shadows. He groaned and took a step back to lean back on a desk. I followed him and pulled down his boxers, staring at him with my mouth parted.

"You're big."

"S-shut up, Princess."

I smirked, wondering if he was flustered. I didn't care. He was going to get a lot more flustered in the next few minutes.

His cock had to be the prettiest one I had ever seen. Thick shaft with veins twitching through it and bulbous red head that glistened with pre-cum. I licked it and hummed at the salty taste before wrapping my lips around his tip and sucking him in.

"Fuck, Princess. Y-your mouth..." he grunted, wrapping his hand around my hair and the other on the desk.

My hands wrapped around his shaft and stroked him slowly. I shivered, getting turned on at the sighs and moans he made, arousal seeping out of me as I continued to pleasure him. I pulled away, only to lick the throbbing veins of his cock and kiss the velvety hard skin.

Taking a deep breath, I dipped down and took him in my mouth, moaning and swirling my tongue around his hardened shaft as he jerked his hips.

"I'd give you any fucking thing you want for this dirty little mouth, Princess," he groaned, moving his hips again and trying to hold himself back. "Let me fuck your mouth."

I pulled away, tears glistening in my eyes. Glancing at his face, I said, "No, let me do this." I knew James enough that he wouldn't push it, especially when I slowly fondled his balls, sucking his head again.

I smiled with his cock in my mouth when he rolled his head back and kept changing my name with Princess. Both of his hands were on the desk and I knew he was very close. So I increased my pace and sucked him faster and as deep as I could take him in without gagging. My hands twisted over his shaft and by the low groan, I knew he was about to cum.

"If you don't pull back, Princess, I'm gonna—*fuck*." He sighed, his legs trembling. It was an odd sight to see James so flustered and lose control just because I had my mouth on him.

I knew he'd have my ass for later, but I had to do it.

Just as he was close, I pulled away and stood up. His eyes flashed open, and I knew he was confused, turned on, and angry. I wiped my mouth and licked my lips before straightening my clothes.

"It's my choice if I want to sleep with my dad's best friend, who is twice my age, James." I gritted my teeth and continued, "And for your information, no, he didn't fuck me. I only want one person to fuck me, and you should know that by now."

Opening the door, I left the room with my heart pounding in my ears and my panties soaked.

He's going to kill me.

29
GREEDY PRINCESS

MIA

"**B**low!"

I rolled my eyes with a grin at the innuendo as Summer pestered me. Taking a deep breath, I leaned down and blew over the numbered candles of one and eight that flickered over the pretty chocolate cake with vanilla frosting. Everyone cheered, and it was pure chaos in a few moments when everyone shouted for cake.

A dark figure loomed over me and my breath hitched when he offered me a small smile. "Happy Birthday, Mia." *Not Princess.*

It hurt that he called me by my name and not his Princess.

I nodded, thanking him when he gave me a small present wrapped in pretty red color. His hair was tousled and despite what we had done before, his clothes looked perfect. With no boner or bulge in sight—*boo*.

I parted my lips, but he moved away before I could talk to him, ask him if he had changed his mind or not. I growled at his back and clutched his gift tighter. *He can't avoid me forever.*

Ninety minutes later, we were sitting in my car while he

drove us to the hospital. He hadn't uttered a single word to me when I approached him after the dinner to ask him if he wanted to come with me to meet Dad. It could be because I was shooting daggers at the pretty lady he was smiling at while talking or because I walked mid-way through a blowie.

I hated that I was so jealous of any women who talked to him, touched his arm or even laughed at anything he said. It made my stomach twist with nerves because... we were nothing. He was my teacher, Dad's best friend. I was just a student or an annoying girl he had to take care of. Nothing more.

* * *

"That's a nice bracelet!" Dad beamed, pointing at the dainty jewelry James had gifted me. My smile was tight when I touched the cool diamonds placed over the silver. It was beautiful and made a soft ringing sound when I moved my hand, and I loved it. But James hadn't said a word about it. He was being distant and acting cold towards me.

Only smiling and talking to Clyde as if I didn't exist. I couldn't believe he was making me feel worse about myself on my birthday.

"Thanks. James gifted it to me."

Dad looked better than before, but he still couldn't walk. I chewed on my lip, wondering when he'd be able to come home and have dinner with us or exchange silly gifts.

I blinked back the burning tears when I hugged him at the time of leaving. Visiting hours were over. "I miss you." His arms squeezed me before he pulled away, his eyes glittering.

"I miss you too, Pumpkin." He smiled and glanced over my shoulder at James. I looked away and walked out of the room, clutching the gift box in my hand. I knew what it was because I had seen him carving it. A small wooden elephant that had a big smile. I clutched it to my chest.

"Let's go."

I didn't reply and followed him to the parking lot. Each of our steps echoed in the night's silence. My heart felt heavy at the distance between us. He'd be joking and holding me close by now, like he did after every visit to the hospital.

"James."

His eyes were dark and piercing when they landed on my face. "Sit."

I swallowed the lump in my throat and obeyed, sitting down on the passenger seat. Somehow, he seemed large and intense when he drove us to the house, but he was calm when we entered the house, turning on the dim lights in the living room.

"Come here."

I jumped hearing his rough tone and looked at James. He was sitting on the couch with his long legs spread out, the veins on his forearms tensing as he slowly unbuttoned the few buttons on his shirt, sliding his large palm on his thighs. His face was covered in shadows, his ocean blue eyes were so dark they seemed onyx. He looked like a beast who hadn't eaten in days.

"No, thanks." I moved towards the stairs, ready to spring upstairs—

"I wasn't asking, Mia," he said gently, making me freeze. "Come. Here."

I didn't move, my fingers twisting on the bracelet he gifted me. *What's the worst thing that can happen?* He could tease me for a few hours and not make me cum. But I had a toy that I could use—

"Five."

I sputtered, turning around, "You can't do that!"

He ignored me, titling his head. "Four."

My heart beat increased and I could feel the nerves in my body bubbling up and anxiety settling in. *What is he going to do?*

"Three."

My lips fell apart. "James…"

"Two."

"What are you going to do, Daddy?" I stayed rooted. "Fuck me?"

Yes, I was serving my ass to him on a silver platter, but it felt good—*powerful*—to see a flicker of emotion in his cold eyes.

"One." He stood up, and I backed away. "Yes, my little bratty slut, I'm going to fuck you."

With a small smile spreading on my lips, I ran. My breathing was harsh, my feet padding on the floor when I climbed up the stairs, fear and something raw and scary and hot rolling through me when I heard him follow me, his pace quicker. *Of course, he is quicker than me.* He had the advantage of longer legs and stronger muscles from years of working out in the gym for four days a week.

"Got you."

I squealed when his hand wrapped around my wrist, pushing me to the wall and trapping me against it. Panting, I tried to squirm and wriggle away, but whenever I tried to move, he was there, inching up and closing over me until all I could breathe was *him*. Pine and male scent.

"Look at me, Princess," he said, his voice low, still holding me against the wall with his hand on my wrists. *Why won't he touch me?*

"What?" I snapped. Well, I tried to, but it sounded more like a breathy whisper.

"You want this?" he asked, his eyes sincere and soft even though his hold was firm.

I nodded, despite knowing the risks. I ached for him.

Couldn't he see that? "Please... God, please, Daddy."

James moved closer. "Hm? Please, what?"

His eyes darkened, jaw clenched as his hand cupped my cheek. He was going to... I could see it in his eyes.

I licked my lips. "Fuck me."

He rumbled, "This mouth."

I gasped when he slid his index finger inside my mouth, pressing against my body, so close and so tight that my breasts pressed over his chest, his hard length rubbing against my thigh.

"Ask nicely," he ordered, another finger sliding inside my mouth as I sucked them. My frown must have given me away as he pressed his fingers down on my tongue, "I said ask me, nicely, brat."

"Please fuck me, Daddy." I burned with embarrassment when muffled words came out of me with his fingers inside me, stretching my lips and toying with my tongue. Yet my underwear was damper than ever.

"Such a good girl." He pulled out his fingers and slammed his lips on me, my head pressing against the wall as I groaned at the bite of his teeth on my bottom lip. I was melting in his arms and being putty when he kissed me deep, moving his lips and tongue like he was fucking me. I burned everywhere he touched, hoisting me up in his arms as I frantically tried to rub against him, holding his shoulders.

"Greedy Princess," he groaned, throwing me down on the bed. I gasped, flying in the air and feeling the comfortable sheets of my bed. He threw me. Before I could scold him, he was upon me, closing his mouth on me and pressing me down on the bed with his weight.

"Want me to fuck your pretty little cunt, Princess?" he crooned, rubbing his fingers over my shorts.

"Y-yes, Daddy," I gasped, pushing my hips on his hand and grinding on them.

30
TIED UP

MIA

I opened my eyes when James pulled away, looking at me with such intense eyes that I had to hold down a shiver. He tentatively looked at me, licking his lips. I squirmed underneath his heavy gaze and reached up to him.

"No." His frame loomed over me, his fingers unbuckling the belt on his pants. "I'm gonna take my time today, okay, Princess?"

I nodded, too entranced by his long fingers and strong thighs straddling me and lazily pulling the leather belt out of the loops. My mouth ran dry when his hand reached down and squeezed my waist.

"I need answers, brat." His tone was dark. "Use your little mouth."

Swallowing, I met his eyes and said, "Y-yes, Daddy."

"What's your safe word?" James asked, leaning up and holding my wrists down on the mattress above my head. I squirmed more. Gasping when he pressed his weight over my stomach, glaring at me. "Quit moving and answer me. What's your safe word?"

"Peach," I breathed.

"That's right." His jaw was clenched when he looped the belt around the metal bedpost and over my wrists, binding them. My breathing got heavier. "And when do you use that safe word?"

"I-I..." I scrambled, frowning at him, "When I want to stop?"

His hand cupped my cheek, and he smiled at me, "Yes, sweet Princess. And when it hurts."

"W-what hurts?"

"Anything at all, okay?" He tilted my head. "Can I trust you to say it, Mia?"

"Yes, Daddy." My voice was shaky when I replied, "I'll say it if it hurts or I want to stop."

"Such a good girl." James rewarded me with a sweet kiss. It was sloppy and messy, making my heart flutter and head dizzy. I wanted to touch his face. My wrists tugged at the knot he made, a whimper eliciting out from my throat when I couldn't move them.

"Mmm," he rumbled, pulling away, gliding his hands underneath my tee shirt. "I'm going to make you cry a little, okay, Princess?"

"M-my hands... James—*Daddy*," I corrected quickly, tugging again, but it wouldn't budge. I was tied up, alone, and at his mercy.

He smiled again. But it was deliciously wicked. "I like them tied up, Princess, you don't?"

I shook my head, gasping when his hand slid down my shorts, rubbing me through the soaked panties.

"Liar," he crooned, circling my clit and making my back arch. "Your pussy is sopping wet, my pretty little slut. Admit it. You like being tied up and punished by Daddy, *hm*?"

I groaned and panted through his ministrations, drowning in the warm glow that spread all over me and was ready to burst. But he pulled away before I could orgasm, making me cry out and yank at my bound wrists harder.

"P-please, Daddy. I want to cum. Fuck me." I didn't care I was babbling or outright begging him, but I was wet and desperate to feel him inside me. And by the look of the boner tenting his pants, he was, too.

"Shh, sweet slut." He ran his hands through my tee shirt and scrunched the fabric on each side. "Let me take my time with you." My mouth fell apart when he yanked, tearing the fabric and throwing off the shreds, eyeing my poking nipples through the bikini he had bought for me.

He cupped my breasts, molding them in his large palms and pinching the hard nubs. "I'm going to edge you until you're a crying, wet mess, Princess. Until you forget your name and beg me to fuck you."

"James..." I cried out when he leaned down and sucked on my sensitive nipple through the bikini. Licking it and biting it. "P-please touch me."

"My little slut wants more, hm?" he teased, untying the bikini and baring my breasts to him. My cheeks turned hot under his roving gaze and I wanted to hide away. With my hands tied up against the headboard, my chest was stretched out, my pebbled nipples poking the air. "I love your perky tits, Princess. Look how gorgeous they are. *Fuck*."

My eyes widened, feeling his hard on rubbing against me when he kneaded my breasts. I had always considered myself a proud member of the itty-bitty-titty community and never thought they were any man's wet dream, but seeing James lose his control at the sight of them twice in twenty-four hours made me want to go topless every time I'm with him.

James didn't just like my breasts, he worshipped them. Moaning and rutting against my spread legs while he kissed them. Sucking my nipples, biting them, pinching and placing hickeys all over.

I wish he hadn't tied up my hands so I could touch him, hold his thick hair as he worshiped my body, his large hands caressing me gently and softly even though his words were down right filthy.

I was sweating and desperate when he lowered to unzip my shorts, slowly sliding them off from my legs leaving me naked except the bikini bottom on the bed. I took a sharp intake of breath, seeing him look at me like that.

"*My...*" he whispered, rubbing his bottom lip and smirking, "Don't you look ravaging."

A small whimper tore out of me, making me wriggle and hide myself, closing my legs and shying away from his penetrating gaze. He chuckled, slowly undoing his buttons and removing his shirt. I eyed his muscled chest, clenching myself when I noticed how hard he was.

"You're lucky I'm not tying your legs." He purred, crawling up my legs and settling between them, his hands stroking my calves and thighs. His eyes drifted from my legs, my stomach, breasts to my face and asked softly, "Are you ready to cry for me, my little princess slut?"

"C-cry?"

"Mhmm, begging and whimpering with your sweet moans until you are nothing but a drippy little mess." I took a shuddering breath when he teased me through the fabric that covered my heated sex. "My drippy little mess. I've to prep you up before I take you, no?"

"Prep?" My eyes widened. "I-I can take you."

"Hm, I like the enthusiasm, but I don't want to hurt you." He pulled away, a dirty smirk on his lips. "Well, I want to hurt you... but not like that."

"Hurt me like what?"

"Don't worry, Princess." He placed a soft kiss on my hipbone, tugging off the bikini and whispered, "You'll find out soon enough."

31
LOOK AT ME
MIA

I gasped when he flipped me around, my hair falling on my sides as James settled me on my knees, pressing his hand on my back until I was arched up to him. I shivered because I was bare and he could see everything.

"Look at that..." he rumbled, his cool breath brushing against my sensitive lips. "My Princess has such a pretty pink pussy. Already wet for me, hm, baby?"

I moaned when he touched me. Tracing a soft line from my clit to my slicked lips. When he did it again, I tried to move away because all the sensations were spreading across my lower body to my head.

A sharp burn spread across my ass, making me tug at my bound wrist again. James soothed the burn and said in a much more serious tone, "You know the safe word, Princess. Use that or stay still and let me play with you."

I stayed still, biting my lip when he spanked me again, using his other hand to rub my clit, slowly teasing me. He continued praising me when I moaned, feeling his finger slide inside me. I was holding on to the leather belt as I shook, the warmth of releasing all the pleasure just on the brink.

But he pulled away, making me whine and spanking me two times on each cheek.

"Please, Daddy." I looked over my shoulders, "I want to cum so bad!"

My breath hitched in my throat when he spread my legs wider and leaned down. "You will, Princess. Just not yet. Daddy wants to play with you how you played with him, *hm?*"

I swallowed the lump in my throat. He was definitely punishing me.

I held back a shiver when his thumb parted my nether lips, groaning against my sensitive skin before covering my pussy with his mouth. I couldn't hold back my moans when he used his tongue to lick me like his favorite ice cream. Sucking the clit and edging me with his hot mouth until I was dripping down my thigh and begging him.

After what felt like hours, he pulled away once again when I was on the brink of an orgasm, making me sob.

"Oh, no you don't, pretty slut. I'm gonna keep going for a little longer. If you can hold back, I might let you cum, hm?" His fingers slid inside me easily and I clamped them tightly, trying to grind on them when he spanked my burning ass once again. "Think you can do it, sweet girl?"

"*Hnngh.*" I had clearly lost the ability to speak after moaning and groaning for so long. Even my throat felt sore.

Spank.

"Answer."

Spank.

"Me."

Spank.

I whimpered, "Y-yes, Daddy."

"Good girl," he murmured his praise before licking me

once again. I relaxed on the bed or I tried to with my wrists tied to the bedpost and being on my knees while James kept lightly spanking my ass and inner thighs when I tried to snap them closed.

He was right. I was begging and desperate for him to fuck me after being played for so long.

"What's that?" he asked, pulling away and flipping me on my back and straightening me up. "You said something, Princess?"

I glared at him through my wet lashes, ready to start crying if he didn't fuck me. "I-I said I'm sorry."

"*Sorry...*"

"I'm sorry, Daddy."

"Sorry for what?"

I sputtered, "Sorry for playing with you." After another breath, I whispered, "Please don't be mad at me."

He narrowed his eyes and hovered above me, his face inches away as he whispered, "I'm not mad at you, sweet girl." He softly caressed my cheek, wiping away the leaking tears. "I'd never play with you if I was mad. I didn't want to fuck you because you should be with someone who's your age."

"But?"

"But I'm too fucking selfish." James smiled, tracing his thumb over my lip. "I'm going to fuck you, Mia."

My lashes fluttered, "P-please."

He made a quick work to undo the knot and checked my wrists as soon as the belt fell. He kissed the red hues and even massaged my arms, asking me if it hurt anywhere. I just shook my head and let him take care of me. He could've kept me tied up and fucked, but he needed me to touch him and soothe him just as much as I needed him.

So I did. Caressing his cheek, I leaned closer until our lips met. I moaned when he pressed his hot body over me, covering me on the bed until we were touching everywhere.

My hands curled over his hair while he embraced me. I whimpered and squirmed, feeling his hard member rub over my thigh. I slid my hand between us and rubbed him over his pants.

"Fuck, Princess," he groaned, thrusting in my hand. "I need to fuck you now."

I licked my lips and watched him as he shucked off his pants and boxers, standing naked at the edge of the bed. My throat bobbed as I looked at his length, two prominent veins around his thick girth and angry red head with a leaking bead of glistening pre-cum.

My mouth went dry. "W-we won't fit."

He chuckled and settled himself between my legs, tearing a foil packet. "We will, Princess." His eyes flashed at me, giving me a dirty smile, "You were begging for my cock moments ago. I'll make sure we fit."

I nodded shakily watching him roll on the condom. I almost moaned when he pumped himself. He was too fucking hot.

"Keep looking me like that and I'll cover your pretty tits with my load."

"No," I shook my head despite how much I liked the sound of it. "Fuck me, please, Daddy."

Stroking my knee, he rubbed his tip over my wet slit making me bite my lip at the anticipation. My eyes raked over the vee of his hip bones to the way his abs tensed when he kept teasing me. The clench of his jaw was delicious, and it ticked when the head of his cock slid inside me.

A cry erupted from my throat and I instinctively closed my legs. I could feel him pulsing inside me—

"*Shh*, Princess," he murmured softly, slowly rubbing my clit with his thumb and looking at me without moving an inch. "Relax. You can take it, sweet girl."

I nodded shakily, following his breathing and relaxing my

walls. This was James, he'd never hurt me. He even gave me a way out and I knew it in my heart that if I said the word at that moment, he'd stop, clean me up and cuddle me to sleep. As much as I liked that idea, I wanted him inside me.

"Pl... *ease*. More," I sputtered with a gasp and tried to buck my hips against him, feeling the girth stretching my walls.

His fingers slid over my waist as he leaned down to suck on my breast, taking a nipple in his mouth and biting it. "Have patience," he whispered hotly and pulled away to flick his dark blue eyes at me. With an experimental roll of hips, he gave a small thrust that made my head fall back. I could feel his shaft gliding inside me. No wonder he had edged me for so long. He wanted me soaking so I could take him.

"You like it?"

"I... like it." I covered my face when I made another lewd noise at his fullness. It stung because he was big, but it also felt weird... a good kind of weird.

"Don't cover your face. Look at me," he grunted, moving his fingers faster over my clit. "Look at me while I fuck you, Princess."

My face heated as I placed my hands beside me, scrunching the sheets underneath me and meeting his handsome face.

"Good girl," he whispered and slowly sunk inside me.

Sparks flew behind my lids as I clamped around his full length settling inside my pussy. It was too much. After playing with me for almost an hour, I was strung up and feeling his full length throbbing inside me, filling me to the hilt, made me see stars as shivers of pleasure rolled through me with his name on my lips.

32
SAY PLEASE

JAMES

I groaned, feeling the spasms of her pussy around my dick. She was cumming so fast and so hard that it was a miracle I hadn't shot my load.

Her lashes fluttered, and she made small little moans as I soothed her shaking little body, tucking her hair behind her ear and smoothing my hands over her legs. I'd stay still as long as she'd want me to. I wanted her to be comfortable.

"That's my good Princess." I leaned down, kissed her, sighing in relief when she clung to me, wrapping her arms around my neck and pulling me closer.

"How'd you feel, Mia?" I asked, trailing my kisses down her neck to ignore my aching balls. I wanted to rut inside her until they were empty.

"F-full." Her cheeks turned redder as she grabbed my shoulder and looked at me with wide eyes that gleamed with tears. "Move, James. Please."

I grumbled in approval and slowly retreated, clenching my hand on the sheet to hold myself back from plunging inside her wet heat again and again. *Slow, James. Take it slow.*

Keeping my eyes pinned on her face, I slowly thrusted inside, her sex clenching me as her lips parted.

"M-more," she demanded, her fingers sinking on my shoulders.

"Whose pussy is it, Princess?" I grunted, slamming inside her, feeling her legs tremble around my waist. "Hm? Who does this pussy belong to?" I asked, rubbing her sensitive clit.

Her hazel eyes gleamed as she gasped out, "Y-you."

"Say. It." I demanded, thrusting after speaking each syllable.

"You, James!" she cried out, her skin glowing with a red flush and sweat. "It belongs to you, Daddy."

"That's right," I whispered, rewarding my princess with a soft kiss, slowing my pace but hitting deeper and harder to rub against her g-spot. "It's mine. Are we clear?"

"Mhmm. Yes, Daddy."

"Good girl," I muttered in the crook of her neck, tightening my hold on her waist. "Such a good girl. I'm going to make you cum again, hm? My sweet princess slut deserves more orgasms."

I chuckled when her walls clamped me hearing my dirty words whisper against the shell of her ear. Pulling back to look at her face, I considered myself the luckiest person that Mia chose to have sex with. Trusted me enough to be so open and vulnerable. *I wanted to protect this girl.*

Noticing my expression, her arms tightened around my nape and pulled me closer to kiss her. I hummed, swallowing her soft moans and licking her bottom lip.

No. She's mine. Others would use and exploit her. I'd keep her safe. I'd take care of her. I'll do whatever she tells me to.

"Please, Daddy," she whispered, her legs quivering as my pace quickened.

I strummed my fingers faster over her little bundle of nerves and held her close when she exploded beneath me in another wave of orgasm. My balls tightened, feeling the tightness of her heat, my hips jerking faster, trying to ride out her orgasm as long as I could before letting out a low groan and spilling inside her.

My eyes squeezed shut as I kept plunging and pushed my cock deep until I hit the hilt and stayed there. My shoulder drooped, and I fell over her, keeping my weight off of her body and nuzzling my face between her breasts. *Fuck me.* My balls were empty and dick was sensitive, but I've never felt so good after an orgasm. I could feel the sharp burn on my back where she must have scratched me and smirked, kissing her soft skin.

"You okay, Princess?" I asked, my voice hoarse. I peered from her chest, stroking her shivering body and slowly releasing her legs as she blinked at me from her half-lidded eyes.

"I need…" I straightened up, waiting for her to complete her sentence. I would give her any fucking thing she wanted. She took a deep breath and said, "I need a minute."

Worried, I slowly pulled out and seeing her frown, my heartbeat increased. *What the fuck? Did I hurt her?* I checked her body for any bruise and even between her legs—

"*Stop.*" Mia tried to wave me off when I spread her legs and checked her pussy, bending down. "What are you doing?" she squeaked out when I slid my finger over her sensitive folds with furrowed brows.

"You didn't even bleed. Are you hurt?" I demanded, cupping her cheek. "Does it hurt anywhere? Did I hurt… you?"

If I did, I was ready to chop my hand after taking care of her.

"You didn't." Her cheeks flushed deeper, and she shook her head. "You didn't hurt me, Daddy."

Her sweet whisper relieved me, but I still needed to know if she was okay. "Then?"

"I just needed a minute to form words."

I blinked at her. Pursing my lips when she covered her face with embarrassment. But I was too proud of myself to not smirk and tease her about it.

Prying her hands off of her flustered face, I whispered, "Did I fuck you so good that you forgot how to think, Princess?" Her cheeks turned redder. "Did Daddy fuck you that good, hm?"

"You're embarrassing me."

"You love it. Don't move." I kissed her forehead and left her on the bed, making my way to her ensuite. Removing the condom, I cleaned myself and took a wet washcloth back to her room. My heart stuttered seeing the sight of her on her queen-size bed, and I wanted to fuck her again.

"I can do it myself." She sat up and tried to bat my hand away, but my grip tightened on her leg.

"Good princesses let their daddies take care of them. Let me." I gave her a stern look and gently cleaned her, making sure she wasn't bleeding or had any bruise.

"Does it hurt anywhere?" I asked again, kissing her knee for being so well.

Mia squirmed when I pulled back. "I feel sore."

That won't do.

"Stay here." I ordered and started the bath in her washroom. Checking if the water temperature was lukewarm with my hand, I added one of her scented oils in it. I found her lids getting heavy with sleep as she yawned and stretched her limbs. She smiled at me when I picked her up, pressing her closer before sinking into the bathtub.

"Are we going to braid each other's hair now?" She giggled when I washed her hair, shampooing it gently, massaging her scalp well.

"We'll do anything you want, Princess," I murmured, cleansing the shampoo and applying conditioner because I knew how crazy she was about it. She had once lectured me in the grocery store why shampoo and conditioner were much better than the two-in-one which I always bought. I had bought the two different bottles just to see her grin.

"Anything, Daddy?" she asked teasingly and looked over her shoulder, wriggling her ass over me.

I tugged her hair, making her gasp and whispered in her ear, "If I fuck you again, you won't be able to walk for a while, brat. So be a good girl."

She turned away, and I knew she was pouting without seeing her face. I ignored it and washed her body with her cherry scented body wash, rubbing her everywhere with the foaming washcloth and letting her do the same to me. Her pout slowly disappeared when she straddled me to wash my hair, ordering me to keep my eyes closed because I kept making heart-eyes to her breasts, her words, not mine.

"James?" she whispered when I squeezed her bum for the last time after applying the chamomile lotion.

"Hm?" I took a clean towel and patted it over her damp hair, looking for a hairdryer.

"James." Mia's voice was much firmer, and I turned to meet her eyes in the mirror. Her pupils were dilated, and she was squirming. "I-I want to do it again."

I dropped the towel and pressed her to the counter. "Say please, pretty Princess."

33
BOY TROUBLE

MIA

I wiped the counter. It didn't feel right, so I sprayed some cleaner and wiped it again, applying more pressure. The sweet, sugary scent of vanilla and caramel wafted in the air. My neck prickled with perspiration. It wasn't right—

I jumped, almost dropping the cleaner and wipe when I heard the oven ding. The cinnamon rolls were done. But my stomach was still twisted with nerves. Leaning back on the counter, I checked my phone when it vibrated with a message notification.

Summer: im bord
Me: Hi Bord, I'm Mia!
Summer: haha vfunny. can i come over
Me: sure, ask em too. I made cinnamon rolls.
Summer: uhoh :)

I frowned at the little creepy smile and kept my phone aside. I took a sharp breath when I bent over to pull out the tray of the cooked rolls. There was an odd twinge between my legs because I had turned ravenous after having sex for the first time and couldn't sleep until James had fucked me to sleep.

My cheeks heated remembering the night before. How filthy, yet gentle, he was. Washing me, taking care of me, making me orgasm so many times that I was feeling sore. I had pouted when he had to leave early in the morning to check up on some things and meet up with his assistant. Despite handing over his company, he still made sure everything was going well. He even had a meeting with his accountant (yes, on a Sunday) so I had dozed off on the fresh sheets.

The house felt empty without either James or Dad, and it made my heart trip because I was already missing them. How would Dad react when he finds out? *Wait*. Will my dad ever find out? Will I tell him about James?

I was thankfully saved from my overthinking by a bell and walked over to open the main door and let Summer and Emma in. Summer was grinning as she enveloped me in a hug, screaming 'I missed you!' despite only having been apart for a few hours, while Emma looked like... Emma. White ribbon in her blonde curls, white almond-shaped nails, and a prefect attire to attend an 80's rich party.

"Did you use a new moisturizer?" Emma asked, squinting at me and poking my cheek.

I touched my cheek and frowned. "No?"

"You're glowing," she replied and smiled at me. "It suits you."

I'm glowing? I swallowed the lump in my throat and tried to bat off the heat creeping up my neck. I didn't know sex-glow was a thing.

"First, show me the rolls and then tell us about your boy trouble."

"What boy trouble?" I opened the cabinet shelf and pulled

out plates for them while they settled on the stools, looking at the glazed cinnamon rolls with heart-eyes.

"You never make cinnamon rolls," Em said, looking at them pointedly. "Unless you have a boy trouble."

"I don't do that." I frowned, serving the rolls and crossing my arms. "I make cinnamon rolls."

"No, you don't. The last time you made them was a year ago when that guy from PE asked you out—oh this is so fugging goof," Summer said with a mouthful of food while Emma took a small bite and chewed, swallowed, patted her lips with a napkin, and looked at me.

"You also baked them when Aaron asked you out on a Halloween date," she answered.

I blinked at both of them. *I stress bake cinnamon rolls?!*

"So spill. What's the boy trouble?"

I thought about James and shook my head. He was definitely not a boy or a trouble—unless I brat out.

"It's nothing." I cleared my throat and looked anywhere but at their eyes. "I think I got over stress baking—anyway, do you wanna watch a movie or swim?"

Summer shared a look with Em before piling another roll onto their plates. I made a huge batch so I could take it to the hospital for Dad and his sweet nurses. I checked my phone for any notifications as we went upstairs to watch a movie in my room.

James: I'll be late. There might be leftover lasagna and your birthday cake. Eat your dinner on time.

Me: Yes, Dad

James: ...

James: You forgot something, Princess.

I rolled my eyes and typed out a reply 'Yes, Daddy' before looking up at the scene in my room. It didn't look like I had sex, but my friends had sharp eyes.

Emma frowned, clutching her stomach. "I think I might've gotten my periods."

Summer and I cooed at her as she went to my ensuite. If she had started hers, then mine would be in a week or so. I was sprawled with Summer on the bed when Emma opened the door to the washroom, her face pale, and called for me.

"What is it?" I asked, concern lacing my voice. "Does it hurt too much? I've a heating pad—"

"I saw a condom in the bin."

My eyes widened as she held my arm and walked us out of the room into the hallway. "Why do you have a condom in your bathroom, Mia?"

I crossed my arms and sputtered out, "I-I'm eighteen."

She narrowed her sharp eyes. "It was a used condom, M."

I pursed my lips and before I could utter, Summer joined in the conversation. "Did someone pop Mia's cherry? On her eighteenth?" She was beaming. "Did you have a birthday sex? I'm so happy and jealous!"

The only response I could voice was a sad little noise from the back of my throat.

"Who was it?" Emma asked, touching my arm. "It's okay if you don't want to tell us, but was it okay?"

I saw stars, Emma.

I took a shaky breath and replied, "I-it was. I'm sorry I can't tell you who it was, but I promise I took care of myself—he took care of me and it was… great." *It was out of this world.*

"By the flush on your cheeks, we can imagine, M." Summer nudged my shoulder and wriggled her brows, "At least give us a hint. Was he at the pool party?"

I nodded, and she whopped before holding both of our hands with wide eyes.

Emma looked at me and asked, "Does James know?"

"Huh?"

"Does he know you had sex?" She raised a brow. "I know he's staying here."

I swallowed the lump. *Yes, Emma. He knows I had sex because he was present the entire time, edging me with his dirty words, fingers and mouth and then fucking me into the mattress until I was unable to think for a few moments.*

Thankfully, Summer saved me. "You know what? It's time to celebrate."

"Summer, no."

"Yes!" she replied and grinned at Emma, who looked like she was actually considering partying. "Don't you have those tickets for the new club? What's it called? Vixen? We should go there!"

"Guys," I tried to interrupt their plan. "We have school tomorrow."

"Uh-huh and your point, miss I-am-not-a-virgin-anymore? When was the last time all three of us went clubbing?"

The silence made Summer purse her lips, her curly hair falling across her shoulders as she gave both of us a pointed look.

"Can't we stay in and watch Heath Ledger serenade Julia Stiles while stuffing our face with carbs?"

Emma considered it for a moment. I was giving her my best puppy eye look while Summer was offering her best smirk. It was an unfair advantage because I must have looked constipated while she looked like a goddess.

"Summer is right." I groaned, but Emma continued, "We haven't celebrated in a while. It should be fun."

"What about school?" I grumbled.

"It'll be fine."

"What about... Caleb?" I tried.

Emma's eyes sharpened. "I don't care what he thinks. He

still hasn't apologized. I want to go clubbing with my friends who care about me. *Not* him."

"Great! I've the fake IDs ready, we just need to turn you from I-am-a-sweet-baker to I-am-the-baddest-bitch." Summer dragged me back to my room and planted me on the bed while she rummaged through my wardrobe.

I picked at my floral skirt and cute top. "What's wrong with a sweet baker look?"

Summer tutted as she roved her gaze over me. "Nothing's wrong if you were invited to a kids' birthday party. But we are going to a club that's named Vixen, sweetheart. We need to dress up for it."

Emma offered, easing my worry. "How about both? A baker that looks like a vixen?"

I stood up. "I have the perfect dress for it."

34
SEX WIZARD

MIA

An hour later, all three of us were getting out of a cab dressed like we were going to walk on a red carpet. I had donned the lilac purple dress, its expensive soft fabric hugging my waist before flowing into a soft skirt that reached my mid-thigh. I had slipped into white sandal heels and applied minimal makeup with red lips. I looked and felt pretty. And as Summer had called me, 'A sexy baker who's the baddest bitch.'

Emma was still wearing her attire from before, with a short skirt and blouse, with sharper makeup. Summer had changed into one of my corsets that I never wore because I felt too shy, which looked great over her dress.

The club was located out of the city and near an abandoned road. Despite that, the crowd queuing up with sparkling clothes seemed excited, and the energy was intoxicating.

Our IDs were in hand, and, as usual, I let my friends handle talking with the intimidating guard when he checked them and flashed the light over the three of us.

"Are you here for the opening?" he grumbled.

Emma flicked her hair over her shoulder and crossed her arms as if she was in a hurry. "Yes. It's mentioned in the tickets."

"It'll be packed tonight." He gave us back our IDs and opened the dark velvet curtain. "Enjoy the show, ladies."

I shivered and stepped inside, clutching my friends' arms on each side. The air smelt like a sharp, exotic perfume in the dark hallway that led to another curtain. I had to blink to get adjusted to the neon lights that flashed around the vast expanse of the club.

My mouth fell seeing the two stories of the club hidden in the shadows but illuminated with golden lights as if we were in some exotic, luxurious mansion and not a club. Even the music vibrated through the walls, making the hairs on my nape stand up with goosebumps. It made me dizzy, and I wanted to join the people on the stage and dance with them, run my hands over my body—*shit*. I felt like touching myself in front of a crowd, and I had just entered the club.

"Holy shitballs," Summer breathed, squeezing my hand as we made our way to one of the empty circular booths sitting in the corner covered in deep red velvet. "This is amazing. Did you know the club would be like this?"

Emma shook her head but made herself comfortable against the expensive leather seat. She fit right in while Summer and I were gaping at our surroundings. Even though I felt out of my comfort zone, it felt somehow right. Especially after James' class, I could notice the subtle lighting and how an audience would move in such a space. The designer had done a splendid job of creating an almost erotic experience for each person.

"There's no information about the club online, and even their Instagram is sparse with very little details," Emma said as we scrolled through the iPad placed in front of us with a variety of alcohol and snacks and even rooms. I was still gaping at it when she clicked through the cocktails and ordered three for us. "It's apparently invite only, and you can upgrade your membership. Do you want to eat anything?"

"Even I'm not rich enough to eat a taco for twenty dollars," Summer scrolled through the other snack options and selected nachos instead. She turned to Emma and said, "How the hell did you grab invitations for such a club, anyway?"

Emma stiffened, pursing her lips. Despite her cold poker face, I noticed her brow twitch. "I'll pay—"

I stopped her. "You got us the tickets. I can pay for the drinks and snacks."

Neither of them complained as I added my credit card details. The tempo of the song changed, and I shuffled in my seat, craning my head to look around when some announcement was made. Emma was scrolling through her phone while Summer was tapping her fingers on the table.

"I want to look around."

"I want to dance."

Summer and I said in unison, making Emma sigh and both of us grin. Before we could stand and go to the dance stage, our drinks and snacks were served by a very hot server dressed in a crisp shirt, slacks, and bowtie. Yes, a freaking bowtie. Even his hair was gelled back. He winked at us as he kept our tray, silver rings on all of his fingers.

"This is delicious." I smacked my lips at the tangy taste and took another big sip of the cocktail. I hadn't checked what Emma had ordered, but I trusted her judgement. Before I knew it, I had downed the drink and was walking towards the dancing crowd on the stage. My skin felt warm underneath the lights, being surrounded by smiling couples and girls grinding on each other, laughing as they even shared a kiss.

Soon, Summer and Emma joined me as we let our hair

loose, swaying to the music and giggling when Summer made a raunchy move, making me blush.

"Hey, are you new here?"

I nodded at the cute guy with blond curls as he closed the distance between us. He was clean shaved and wearing pants and a well-fitted tee. But he wasn't James.

"Sorry, I'm taken." I grinned, waving at Emma and Summer, who waved back.

"Holy shit," the guy stuttered, his cheek turning pink. "Are you girls throuples or some shit?"

"Hey." I frowned, my head buzzing from dancing so much. "We are ladies. And it's called throuple."

"That's so fucking hot," he murmured when my friends stepped closer, sensing that the guy wasn't taking a hint. We had practiced being a throuple or lesbian so many times that it was almost like a second nature to us. More for Summer, as she was bisexual. "Do you all want a male company?"

My frown deepened hearing his tone. *Who the fuck said male company anymore? Who was this guy, anyway?*

Before I could call him off, a cold, low voice said over my shoulder. "Get lost."

My entire body froze hearing that tone, my stomach warming and heart pounding faster when an arm wrapped around me. I peered up from the powerful set of shoulders to the open view of his neck, licking my lips. His jaw was clenching deliciously, and I resisted the urge to tip on my heels and lick it before biting his lips. *God, he is so fucking sexy.* My panties were already dampening just by his mere presence.

He must be a wizard. A sex wizard.

At my thought, he flickered his stony blue eyes at me, his lips twitching.

"Hey man, chill. I was just asking them and they didn't reject me—"

"You can leave. Now." Another voice joined and Emma's face paled.

I saw a stranger standing beside James, his tall frame similar to his with broad shoulders and donning an expensive looking suit and glaring at the blond guy whose face had turned pink receiving the stony expression from him and James. I didn't know who the man was, but I knew he somehow knew Emma, because she swallowed and looked away from his intense stare.

"I didn't think I'd see you here, Princess." My body shivered at hearing the soft, husky voice. "I'm glad you think I'm a sex wizard, though."

Kill. Me.

Kill me now.

35
OR WHAT?

JAMES

Mia's cheeks flushed into a beautiful pink color, looking away and squirming against my arm. I let her go, knowing her friends were present and she wouldn't want us to look too suspicious. I hated that I couldn't even touch her in the public eye. Even holding her hand or leaning too close would be forbidden.

When I left after my meeting with the accountant, I hadn't expected Damon Grant to call me, inviting me to his club on such a short notice. I couldn't deny because Damon was my company's biggest client, and I wanted to see its weekend opening. It had opened the week before, but he wanted to run a few things through in a meeting, which I was more than happy to do. Very few clients did the hands-on work or accepted most of our designs, demanding for a change, while Damon had always been analytical and asked questions.

The last person I wanted to see there after exiting Damon's office on the first floor was Mia. Especially in her lilac dress that looked as if it was made just for her, accentuating her curves and offering a subtle cleavage. I wanted to whisk her away and scold her for coming to such a club without telling me. She wasn't even legal enough to drink, yet I smelled the hint of sweet cocktail in her breath.

"What are you doing here?" Damon snapped, stepping closer to Emma, who tensed underneath his steely gaze.

"It's none of your business," she replied just as coldly, crossing her arms.

Mia nudged me and frowned at me. "I should ask you the same thing. I didn't think you'd be here."

"Am I the only one who's hungry?" Summer asked, looking at all of us.

"We need to talk." Damon didn't ask for Emma's reply before holding her wrist. His eyes flickered to me and Mia. "I'll find you later."

I nodded, watching them disappear into the throng of tipsy crowd. I pinned my eyes on Mia's friend and said, "Order whatever food you want. It's on my tab. I need to speak with her."

With that, I held Mia's hand and dragged her behind me. She was wearing the white sandal heels that were making her slow. I sighed and threw her over my shoulder, ignoring her squeal of protest, and prowled towards one of the rooms in the dark hallway. The guard in shirt and bow tie knew me, so he let me pass through.

"James!" Her fingers pawed at the fabric of my suit. "Put me down. Now!"

"*No.*" I slapped her ass, making her gasp as I kept walking, squeezing her thighs. "I thought I told you to eat lasagna and go to bed."

She growled, "You're not my fucking dad."

I smacked her ass again, closing the door shut behind me. "No, but I'm your Daddy so you do what I tell you to."

"Fuck off," she grumbled, fixing her hair and dress when I sat her down. She was swaying and her cheeks were pink.

I grabbed her jaw, making her look at me. "I'd better watch my mouth if I were you, Princess."

"Or what?" She tried to pull away, even though her hips were trying to grind against me. "You're going to punish it?"

"Do you want me to, sweet slut?" I whispered, nudging my nose against her ear and breathing in her sweet cherry scent. "Because I will. Teaching you how to suck Daddy's cock on your knees until you swallow all of my cum like a good girl, *hm?*"

Her lids fluttered as she pressed against me, her hands tugging at the lapels of my suit. I pulled back, dimming the lights of the room, and let her eyes wander. It was one of the normal ones without any kinky toy collection, but what it lacked in toys, it made up for in the interior. With a raised circular bed in the center of a room, its sheets and mattress custom made with the softest, luxurious silk and hordes of pillows. A soft lace curtain hovered from above, making the bed feel more like a private alcove. The walls were also covered in dark blue wallpaper, a floor-length mirror across the bed with a chest full of condoms, lubes, and soft bondage toys.

"W-what is this?" Mia whispered, trailing her fingers over the blue silk of the bed.

I removed my suit jacket, throwing it on the armchair and removed the cuff links, rolling the sleeves of my shirt over my elbows. Her breath hitched when she looked over at me as I stalked towards her. I tugged her towards me, capturing her lips in a searing kiss, roving my hands over her body until she melted in my embrace. Mia let out the softest whimper, feeling my bulge, and sneaked a hand between us to cup me through my pants.

I growled in her ear, "Kneel if you want my cock, Princess."

She pulled away, her doe eyes wide. I rubbed my thumb

over her chin to wipe the red lipstick that had smeared, knowing it was on my lips as well. I leaned down and licked her neck, kissing the sweet spot below her ear that made her shiver and arch up to me.

"If you want me to fuck you, you'd have to beg for it, sweet girl."

Mia whimpered and pulled away to unbutton my shirt, kissing my throat and licking the hot skin. I let her, throwing my head back and relishing in the little bites of her teeth and scratches her nails made. I smirked, petting her hair as she trailed her kisses to my pecs, kissing my nipples and abs before following the happy trail. I'd mark her twice as much later.

"Good girl." I stroked her cheek when she knelt across me, licking her lips. "Unzip me."

I stopped her hand and ordered, "With your teeth. Keep your hands behind your back."

Her breath shuddered and chest heaved as she squirmed on the dark floor. She looked like an angel with her mussed hair, flushed cheeks, smudged lipstick, and wide eyes. And I was about to taint her more.

"Go on, Princess. You don't want to make your friends wait, do you?"

Her cheeks turned redder, and she leaned forward, capturing the metal zipper between her pearly teeth. I took a sharp breath when she frowned and moved forward before pulling the zipper down. I rumbled when my boner strained against the boxers, her pupils dilating.

My hands threaded through her hair when she licked my length through the fabric, peering her eyes up at me. Fuck. I wouldn't last if she kept going.

"Remove my boxers, Princess. Good girl. Now take me in your mout—*fuck*, that's my sweet slut."

Her mouth was wet and hot and the sight of my length

disappearing past her pouty lips made me want to rut inside her. I held her hair back as she bobbed her head over me, my girth stretching her lips. She pulled back to lick a line through my throbbing sensitive skin, hollowing her cheeks and sucking my tip in her mouth.

"You're taking me so well, Princess." My breathing turned harsh and I could feel my orgasm close, especially when her hands cupped my tight balls, stroking them softly and increasing her pace.

"Stop," I rasped, pulling her head back, a string of saliva following her lips. "Get on the bed. I want to come inside your pussy."

36
ON YOUR FOURS
MIA

I scrambled to my feet, my panties utterly soaked. Before I could strip out of the dress, James cupped my cheek and kissed me. I hummed and pressed closer, wanting to touch him everywhere.

"Keep the dress on," he whispered, pulling at the thin strap and releasing it as it stung my skin. I nodded shakily, the back of my legs hitting the silk of the bed.

"On your fours."

I bit my lip and eyed him. He looked deliciously rumpled, with tousled hair, sexy blue eyes, an unbuttoned shirt that showed off his muscles and his throbbing cock that glistened with pre-cum at the tip.

"Say please."

James smirked and prowled towards me, easily flipping me on my stomach and spanking my cheek before covering me with his length. *"Brat,"* he growled in my ear when I wriggled my ass to tease him, moaning when he pulled my hair, "Shh, Princess. This room isn't soundproof."

I flushed and looked over my shoulder to see him put on a condom. His eyes pinned on me. I tucked my dress over my waist and gasped loudly when he didn't wait to remove my underwear. He tucked it to the side and slid inside me in one harsh thrust.

My elbows gave out, and I moaned into the bed when he retreated, slamming inside me. I was on the brink of an orgasm, but he kept his punishing pace slow and deep, squeezing and spanking my ass. The sounds of our skin slapping against each other and my moans mingled with his low groans echoed in the room.

"Daddy, please," I gasped, clenching him with my walls as he fucked me in a mating press.

"Want Daddy to make you cum, Princess?" he crooned, his kisses soft against my neck while he fucked me into the mattress, making my body jolt with each thrust.

I sobbed, "Yes, please, Daddy!"

"*Fuck*," he groaned and flipped me on my back, capturing my lips in a clumsy, sloppy kiss. His eyes darkened when he straddled me on his lap, topping me from underneath. "Look how pretty you look sitting on Daddy's cock."

I clenched, seeing our reflection in the mirror. My skin was flushed and glowing underneath the dim lights as James continued to pound into me from below, holding my waist and kissing my neck.

"Should I keep you like this, *hm?*" he rasped, holding me down on his length and making me squirm at fullness. My lips fell apart, feeling my juices trickle down his cock. He tucked my hair behind my ear. "Let you cockwarm me for a few minutes until you beg me to ruin you?"

I shook my head, clutching his shoulder, "N-no, I—"

James chuckled, and it was cruel and wicked and so hot that I squeezed him tighter. "You know what I think, Princess?" When I didn't answer, he turned us around so my back was pressed against his chest, and both of us were facing the mirror. "You love it. Your cunt is clenching me so fucking tight. *Look*." He cupped my jaw when I squeezed my eyes shut. "Look at us. Imagine how it'd look to others. Both of us fully clothed with your sweet little pussy cockwarming me. Hm? You like that idea, don't you? Fuck, Princess. You're getting soaked."

I loved that idea. The hem of my dress covered us both and if we were in public, no one would question us, as it seemed like I was just sitting on his lap. I whimpered, squirming on his cock, but there was nowhere else to go. I was so full and stretched out that I couldn't stop squeezing him, trying to grind against him with his hand on my hip.

"Please Daddy, I can't." I tried to fuck myself on him, but he was too strong.

"You can," he whispered, pulling me down on his length, which sent a jolt of pleasure through my entire body making tremble. "Who knew my sweet little princess liked cockwarming so much?"

"Please, please, please fuck me—"

I was going over the edge when he raised my hips and pulled me down on him, slamming his length inside me. I gasped at the full feeling and rode him myself, moving and rolling my hips as much as I could. His groans near my ear were so erotic that I could come just by hearing him, his thighs tightening and his hands squeezed my hips as he kept fucking me.

"Oh, God—"

"I *am* your God," he growled in my ear, wrapping his hand around my throat, keeping his pace, making me explode with pleasure and hold on to him for support.

I don't know for how long I moaned or gasped, convulsing above him, but I could feel his cock pulse before filling the latex with his cum. I whimpered, squeezing him as he rocked us through our orgasm, his lips on my neck.

"My sweet girl," he whispered, caressing my cheek. I

nuzzled into his palm, feeling raw and open. "My good girl. You did so good."

I relished in the warmth of his kiss, his lips soft. His hands stroked over my body, soothing me from the aftershocks until I melted into him, wanting to bury my face in his chest and sleep.

James made me feel so good. Yes, he called me names during the sex, but he always took care of me. Even when I thought I didn't need anyone to look after me, he was always there, asking me if everything was okay and praising me.

My heart pounded at such a flurry of warm emotions that I didn't know when my eyes pricked with tears.

"Let me clean you up—*Mia?* Shit. Princess, are you okay?" He quickly wrapped me up in his arms, his fingers tilting my chin towards him. "Was it too much, sweet girl? Do you want to slap me, curse me?"

I sobbed more, shaking my head and clutching at his shirt. "I... I don't know why I'm crying."

"Oh, *sweet* Princess. You're adorable." His hand stroked my back, his lips brushing against my forehead. "It's okay. Cry it out. I'm here."

"I don't want to cry. I want it to stop."

"It's okay to cry, Princess," he shushed me, petting my hair and stroking my hands and legs as I kept sobbing. "You must have felt intense sensations, so it's natural to let it out."

James didn't move until my sobbing had turned to little sniffles, gently wiping tears off of my face and smiling at me with an odd emotion in his eyes.

"Are you happy?" I asked, my voice hoarse. "I'm crying and you're smiling?"

"You're *so* precious," he chuckled and kissed my nose. "I know I tease you, but god, you need to be protected."

I frowned, crossing my arms.

"*My sweet girl.*" He nuzzled his face closer, kissing my cheek. "You wanna cry more?"

"No! And I don't need protection, nor should I be protected." I gave him a stern look and said, "I should be feared."

His grin widened, making my heart stutter at such a rare sight. He looked so handsome and beautiful when he smiled so openly, his blue eyes sparkling with joy. I wanted to make him smile more. I wanted to be the reason for his happiness.

"Oh yes," he nodded, trying to keep a straight face. "You're very scary."

I hid my face again. "*Shuddap.*"

His chest rumbled with another chuckle, making me smile against his shirt.

PART IV

"I love you as who you are."

37
BE QUIET

MIA

I dabbed my cheeks with a tissue for the last time and took a deep breath when James unlocked the door. He had calmed me down and demanded me to drink water from the bottle he offered. I thought I had creeped him out after sobbing like that, but he seemed closer to me than before, clutching my hand in his palm as we both stepped out of the room.

He had promised that the cleaning crew would clean them and there was nothing to worry about. I trusted him.

"Mia," Emma whispered, her face pale as she looked between me and James. "I... *wait*—are you crying?"

James didn't let go of my hand when I tried to pull away. My heart thundered in my ribs, heat creeping up my neck. I didn't know what to say. She must have already figured everything out.

"No, I-I..." I looked closer at her face, her glistening eyes. "Are you crying?"

She sniffed and looked away. Emma never cried. She was the type of person who'd say 'Oh, well' if she got into a car accident and try to go about her day. Seeing her eyes red and the tears streaked on her cheeks made me concerned.

"Did something happen?" I asked softly, stepping closer to her.

"It's nothing," she snapped and glared at James, crossing her arms. "I knew it was *him*. Did he make you cry?"

"Long answer, no. But short answer, ye—"

I cut him off. "You're not helping."

"Is he taking advantage of you?" Emma demanded, trying to step between me and him. Despite being shorter than me, she still managed to look down at James. It was incredible. *She* was incredible.

"Tell her, Princess," James said, tilting his head and offering my friend a cool look. "Did I take advantage of you?"

My body heated at his teasing words. I held Emma's arm, "He's not, Em. You can calm down."

She clenched her jaw and looked at me, her eyes softening. "I'm interrogating you about this later. I want to get home now."

"I'll drop you off."

Emma glared at James again, but surprisingly, it was ineffective to him. "All three of you had alcohol and I'm taking Mia home, anyway. Come on."

She must be shaken up by whatever had made her cry that she didn't further argue with James. Summer was frowning at her phone and I felt bad about leaving her alone, but when she took one look at me and James, she let out a wolf-whistle.

"You made me fifty dollars rich, M!" She opened her palm at Emma, who scowled and passed her a fifty-dollar bill while I gaped at them.

"Did you put a bet on us?"

"We both knew you had a crush on your hot, dad's best-friend—*hello James*, but when he started teaching at our school and moved into your house, it was as easy as one plus one equals to one scandalous, forbidden romance!" Summer was definitely happy about it.

Emma rolled her eyes. "I thought you'd tell us sooner, considering we are your friends. Summer won because she knew you would be shy about it."

James cleared his throat and tugged at his collar, making my breath hitch. Of course, it was obvious that I had fucked my hot teacher. My red lipstick had smudged his shirt and his neck.

"Shall we leave or you want to eat something more?"

I closed my eyes, praying that we would reach home safely.

* * *

CALLING the drive back home awkward would be an understatement. I kept squirming in the passenger seat for two main reasons.

1. James had torn my panties, and I had to go commando under the dress.

2. My two best friends were silent in the back seats, and I could feel their burning stare on my thigh where James had entwined our hands.

We reached Summer's house first and before she opened the door, she said, "Goodnight. I love you and use protection!"

I covered my face with my other hand and muttered a small 'Goodnight.' Thankfully, neither James nor Emma commented on anything and stayed quiet when we reached her house.

Emma stepped out of the car, straightened her skirt and knocked on driver's window. I held my breath when he lowered the glass.

She gave him a sweet smile and said, "If you hurt Mia, I'll ruin you, Mister James." She tilted her head and blew me a kiss before leaning up and walking towards her manor.

"*Well,*" James said after a few minutes of silence. "That went well."

I groaned and shook my head.

* * *

"MISS MILLER?" My head snapped up from the thick mathematics textbook. One of the school staff leaned into the class as our teacher glared at her for interrupting the class. "Miss Mia Miller?"

"Yes, miss?" I asked nervously, glancing at Summer, who nudged my shoulder.

'You in trouble?' She mouthed, and I shook my head, 'I don't know.'

"Mister James has asked you to stay after school and meet him in his office." She smiled and walked away.

I ignored Summer's teasing and covered my face with hair, hoping no one would notice my flushed face. *Did he have to send a notice to call for me? Couldn't he send me a text like a normal person?* He must have done it to make me anticipate about meeting him. Get me blushing in front of my classmates. *Jerk.*

It had been weeks since Summer and Emma had found out about me and James. As Emma had promised, she had interrogated me the next day, making sure he wasn't isolating me from my family or friends, and gave me the freedom to do whatever I wanted. I was horrified just at the thought of someone ever thinking so badly about James, but my friends were concerned about me, which I appreciated a lot.

They hadn't judged me or him. In fact, Summer confessed

I looked happier with him. Even thinking about it made my heart tight.

After school, when I walked into his office in another building, I wasn't surprised when he bent me over his desk.

"Now be a good girl and stay quiet," he whispered, trailing his fingers over my slicked lips. "Wouldn't want your teachers to know how good I fuck you, hm?"

"Yes, Daddy," I said, pushing my hips back and holding the edge of the desk in front of me. My knuckles turned white when I felt the smooth glide of his head and the soft sting of pain when he slid inside me, stretching me.

"Always so wet for me, my pretty slut," he grunted, grinding into me and covering my mouth when a moan slipped out of me. "Shh. Be quiet. Your moans are for my ears only."

I moaned louder, his hand muffling them as he fucked me with a punishing pace, lowering his other hand to rub my clit. My toes curled in my shoes, each thrust of his cock sending me over the edge as it stimulated the sensitive spot he was accustomed to. James knew exactly where to touch me and with how much pressure to make me cum. The smartass had even recorded it with a timer just to prove me wrong.

"Fuck, Princess." His low groan reverberated in my ear, my orgasm on the edge. "Cum with me. Cum with Daddy."

I nodded, tears sprinting in my eyes as I let go. White hot lust gushed out of me and it expanded into a bigger orgasm when I felt James spill inside me, keeping his thrusts levelled and holding me close when I trembled into more aftershocks. Hot lips met mine, and I greedily kissed him back, whimpering and moaning in his mouth as he held my writhing body close.

"Good girl," he murmured, kissing me once again and pulling out to dispose of the condom. He stroked my back soothingly as I stayed still bent over his desk. My skirt was tucked over my waist and my panties dangled from one ankle.

Just as I was about to straighten up, someone knocked on the door.

38
PROMISE ME

MIA

James tugged down my skirt, sliding papers and books on his desk, which he had pushed down when I had entered his office. I pulled up my panties, straightening my clothes and hair, trying not to panic.

"Enter."

The door opened just as I took a pencil in my hand, staring deeply at the examples of models I had sketched for the final project of the year, which James had asked us to do. I turned around and saw Claire, clutching a sketchbook to her chest, her eyes throwing daggers at me before drifting to James and softening.

"Hi, Mister James!"

Please. I might barf.

"Hello, Clara." James gave her a tight smile when she entered.

"It's *Claire*," she corrected, still smiling prettily at him. Her skirt was inched higher than before. I looked away, squeezing the pencil in my hand. "Are you free? I've a few questions, and I need help with some of my sketches."

She wasn't asking. She was demanding.

"I'll leave." I stood up, picking up my bag and closing the sketchbook. My cheeks heated when I looked at him. His hair was a little rumpled and his face was poker as usual, but the heat in his eyes made me want to crawl back to his lap. "Thank you, um, for your help, Mister James."

I ignored the eye-roll from Claire and left his office with my heart thudding wildly in my ears. I needed to calm down. I didn't care if James had his own fan-following in the school. I trusted him. Even Summer and Emma had noticed how he didn't look at any other women, students, or teachers, whether I was around or not.

With a hand pressed against my cheek, I left the building and headed towards my car. I had finally saved enough to pay Dad's bills. Even though it meant emptying my car and tuition savings, I would be able to take care of my dad. The extra help from Aaron and the other students also helped.

* * *

James

"I'M HOME!" I announced, placing the keys in the fish bowl and stalked towards the kitchen to store the pizza I had bought on the way back. I didn't usually eat pizzas or junk, but Mia deserved it after passing her recent exams with excellent marks. She would wake up early, hunched over her desk when I came back from the gym. I didn't even distract her from her studies, bargaining her with more sex and junk food once the result was announced.

I found Mia sitting by the kitchen bar, staring at her laptop with a dull look on her face. She must've showered by the look of her damp hair. She didn't even dry it? I hope she won't get a cold.

"Everything okay?" I asked, unbolting a few buttons of my

shirt. She didn't even make any exaggerated moaning noises seeing the pizza box. Something was definitely wrong.

She finally looked up, hurt flickering in her eyes. I straightened up, wondering why it was directed at me.

"You didn't tell me," she whispered, her voice hoarse.

Fuck. Did she find out? I didn't want her to find out like this. I wanted to tell her.

"I-I'm sorry, Mia." I squeezed my eyes shut and took a deep breath before looking at her. "I didn't know how to tell you—"

She closed her laptop and stood up. "You could've told me anytime you wanted. But you hid it from me."

"Princess, Mia… it's not easy for me to—"

She threw her hands in the air. "It's about my dad! How is it not that easy?!"

What?

"You paid his bills," Mia said, glaring at me. "You paid all his hospital bills. All of them, yet you didn't tell me."

Oh. She wasn't talking about—

Fuck. Thank God. But I knew I couldn't keep it from her longer. It would be worse if she found out about that from someone else.

"He's my friend, Mia. I did it because I wanted to, and why are you so upset about it?"

"*Upset?*" she asked, her eyes wide. "Upset? I'm not upset, I'm mad, James!"

I kept my tone levelled and asked, "Why are you mad?"

"Because you paid my father's bills!" she sputtered out.

"He's my friend," I repeated. "If Emma or Summer, bless them, got in an accident and couldn't pay the bills, wouldn't you do the same?"

She blinked, considering the scenario, and crossed her arms. "That's not the same."

"Mhmm."

"Stop mocking me."

"I'm not mocking you." I raised my hands. "*Look*. Clyde helped me when I really needed it. When I had no support, emotional, physical or financial. Yet he took care of me, and I wouldn't be standing here if it wasn't for his stubborn determination."

Mia pursed her lips and looked away. I knew she would tear up, but I didn't want to make her cry. I wanted to make her understand.

I crossed the space between us and touched her hand, allowing her to close it around mine as I gently rubbed her knuckles. "If I went through that again, your father wouldn't think twice before helping me. I'm repaying my debt, Mia. It's the least I could do."

Her forest-green eyes peered at me from beneath her thick lashes. Tears were already glistening in them. My heart felt heavy seeing such a pained look on her face, and I couldn't help but wrap my arms around her. She sniffled, tightening her arms around my waist, hiding her face in my shirt.

"*Still*," she said, pulling away and pouting at me. "You could've told me. I saved up for it."

I kissed her forehead. "I know. Now you have more savings for your college."

Mia frowned, shaking her head. "No, it's the tuition fees for the next semester—*you didn't!*"

I shrugged when she pulled away. "You're his daughter, and I promised him I'd take care of you."

"Then take it back. You didn't have to pay my tuition fees."

"I can't. And you've to live with it." I tilted her chin and gently kissed her pout. "I'm not going to apologize for taking care of my Princess. What kind of Daddy would I be if I did that, hm?"

"I-I saved so much, working and—" She quickly shook her head, tipping on her toes and kissing me.

But I pulled away, holding her chin and asking, "Working and what?"

Mia tried to avert her eyes. "It's nothing."

"It's not nothing," I said. "What are you lying about, Princess?"

She looked at me and slumped, knowing I won't let her be unless she tells me. "I… I helped a few classmates."

My voice hardened. "Helped them how?"

"W-writing their essays, doing their homework, that kind of stuff." Pink colored her cheeks, and she looked so vulnerable with her doe eyes, "Please don't tell anyone."

"You did it for money?" I asked, knowing well some of the rich kids would throw money at anyone who would do their hard work.

"Just for Dad's bills," she answered quickly. "Please, James, don't tell anyone. They could get in trouble."

She was worried about them and not about her?

"You can get expelled if you get caught," I said bitterly. I wouldn't let her, though. I had enough material on the entire school board committee that if I threatened enough, they'd make Mia the star student with a scholarship to any Ivy League university she wanted.

"I know, but they would never do that." She bit her lip and added, "Aaron only did it to spend time with me. And others had problems with the subject matter, dyslexia, or needed my help with tutoring."

"Is that why you were staying up so late and waking up early?"

She nodded.

I pulled her closer and ordered her, "Don't you ever do that again. Understand?"

"Y-yes, Daddy."

"Promise me," I demanded. "I don't want you to help your classmates like this. If they need help, let them come to their teachers. If the teachers don't understand, then I'll make them understand, but you are not doing it ever again."

She nodded, licking her lips. "Yes, I won't. I promise."

"Good girl." I leaned down and closed my lips over hers. She sighed, her body relaxing as I coaxed her closer, holding her waist. I deepened our kiss, biting her bottom lip until she moaned, parting them.

"Mia... James."

We both pulled away, seeing Clyde looking at both of us with wide eyes.

39
WELCOME HOME

JAMES

One of the worse things than being caught by their friend while making out with his daughter in his own kitchen was having a fucking boner when it happened.

"*Dad.*" I winced when Mia pulled back, color slashing her cheeks. "You're... you are standing, and you're here?"

I wished I could faint. Or have a heart attack. Anything at that point would work.

Clyde looked like he was having a heart attack or another aneurysm, and I was worried. "Were you just kissing James, or was I seeing things?" Even his voice was barely a rasp, his knuckles tightening on the cane he was holding. Despite staying in the hospital for a couple of months, he looked healthy.

"Would you believe me if I said you're seeing things?" Mia asked, shuffling on her feet.

I took a deep breath and met my friend's eyes. "I was kissing Mia," I answered, keeping my gaze on him, even though guilt and embarrassment made me want to look away. I didn't regret anything. I should have talked to Clyde about it earlier, but I wasn't going to tell him that I liked his daughter when he was sitting on a hospital bed.

"I see." He pursed his lips and limped towards the couch, sitting down. Mia walked towards him, but he shot her a dark look. "Go to your room. I need to talk to James."

Her body tensed and she nodded jerkily before turning away and running upstairs. A moment later, I heard the sound of the door closing. I glanced at him. His face was poker as he pointed at the seat across from him.

"How's your leg?" I asked, sitting down. "I didn't know you were getting released today."

"It's okay." His hazel eyes narrowed. "I was going to surprise Mia and... you, but I wasn't expecting to come home and find my friend pinning my daughter against the kitchen island."

I swallowed audibly, tugging at the collar of my shirt. "I wanted to talk about it—"

"*James.*" His voice turned sharp, and I knew I was talking to an angry father and not my friend. "You promised me you'd take care of Mia. Not kiss her behind my back."

"I *like* her, Clyde."

"You like a girl who's young enough to be your daughter?" His words hurt, making my chest tight and mouth dry.

I couldn't meet his gaze when I asked, "Don't you think I already tormented myself with that question, Clyde? You think I asked for this?" I clenched my fist. "I-I tried to ignore it, but I couldn't."

"She's your student, for fuck's sake!" He ran a hand over his face and I noticed the strain there. The bags underneath his eyes. He looked tired. Exhausted.

I swallowed the lump in my throat. "I tried to fight whatever feelings I had for her, Clyde. But I couldn't. I *can't*. I never intended to keep this a secret from you. I wanted to tell you since the beginning, talk to you about it, but you were in the hospital so I decided to wait until you got back home…"

"What the hell am I supposed to do about this?"

"You should rest." I stood up. "But before that, talk to Mia. I…" I glanced away and added, "I'll go back to my place. Call me if you need anything."

He grumbled something.

I wished I could have pizza with him and Mia, but by the look on his face, it was the last thing he'd have wanted. "And Clyde?"

He finally looked up at me.

"Welcome home." I gave him a small smile before picking up my keys and leaving the house. I could feel the burning stare from the windows, but if I looked at her, I wouldn't be able to leave, so I didn't turn back.

* * *

Mia

"You can't keep ignoring your favourite daughter, who spoils you with sweet, sugary things forever, you know?"

"You're my *only* daughter." Dad rolled his eyes before taking a bite of the healthy and tasty pancakes I made. James was an excellent chef who knew how to make easy recipes, and he had taught me several so I could cook them for Dad. Even thinking about him made my heart ache.

Ever since Dad caught us kissing, Dad had been ignoring me. Even James kept his distance from me at school, and Emma was ready to plan his assassination when she thought he hurt me, because I had been gloomy in the past few weeks.

I pouted, slumping on the kitchen stool, poking the food around. I couldn't ever remember Dad being mad at me or giving me silent treatment. If he made me angry or we had a fight, he'd make up to me by the next morning with zoo tickets or getting me a bunch of stuffed toys. It felt odd not talking to him about random things like the ladybug landing on my palm, how hard PE class was, or Summer being a reckless fool again. It hurt not to smile or laugh with him.

"Do you hate me?" I whispered.

His spoon clattered on the plate and he flickered his eyes at me. His face wasn't cold anymore, but he still looked angry. "You are my Pumpkin, Mia. I could never hate you."

I shrugged, looking away. "This is the first time in two weeks you've looked at me… or said more than three syllables."

He took a deep breath and said, "I'm disappointed."

My eyes stung. "That hurts, Dad."

"Why couldn't you like some other guy?" he asked. "He's twice your age. He's your teacher."

My jaw clenched, hurt turning to anger as I glared at him. "You're making it sound like it's all my fault that I lov—" I shut up and stood up from the stool. "I'll be late for school."

I didn't look at him when I picked up my bag. I felt him stand up and walk towards me before I could turn to the main door.

His hand touched my head. His eyes were soft as he asked, "You love him, Pumpkin?"

I nodded. "I-I know I'm too young to call it love, but he makes me happy, Dad. Even if I get mad at him, he talks to me, and… and it feels warm whenever he's near."

"I'm pretty sure that's called body heat."

I glared at him and crossed my arms.

Dad winced and picked at the knot of my tie which I had done all by myself. "You are growing up fast."

"Yes, Dad."

His eyes gleamed as he ruffled my hair. "I need time, Pumpkin. To feel okay about this."

My eyes lit up. "Really? You… you're not angry anymore? You won't ignore me?"

He looked away, his cheeks turning pink. "Even a blind man can see how much you've grown being with him. Joyce wouldn't be happy with your relationship, but she would never ignore you like I did. I'm sorry, Pumpkin."

I bit my lip at hearing mom's name and hugged him. "It's okay, Captain." I closed my eyes and said, "Mom would scold James."

"She would," he chuckled, petting my hair. "He would be terrified of her."

I pulled back and smiled at him. "Can we do our traditional Saturday dinners again?"

He groaned but agreed, making me squeal with excitement and hug him again. "Come back early today."

"Why?"

"I've booked a doctor's appointment today."

I frowned, checking his legs and at him. "You okay, Dad? I'll come early."

"It's not for me," he shook his head. "I'm taking you to ob-gyn."

My face paled. "Why?"

He gave me a scolding look. "Just because I'm still processing my daughter dating my friend doesn't mean I'm ready to have grandchildren just yet. I'm too young for that—"

"Okay, bye, see you!" My voice was high-pitched when I scampered out of the door, my body heating up. The idea of having a kid with James was too much. But it didn't stop me from wondering if we had a baby. *Would it have my hazel-green eyes or his ocean-blue eyes?*

Grumbling to myself at the silly idea, I drove to the school. I couldn't wait to inform James about the talk with Dad. He'd be very happy.

40
I'M SORRY

MIA

"That's my sweet slut," James rumbled from between my legs, the reverberations of his voice sending shivers of pleasure all over me. "Scream for Daddy."

I threaded my hand through his hair, pulling him closer to my soaked pussy and moaning when he licked me. I squeezed my eyes shut at the flick of his tongue on my sensitive clit. It was too much. Especially after being edged to death in the past hour.

"Daddy," I screamed, my orgasm teetering on the edge. Warm glow spread all over my body, and I kept falling when he slid two fingers inside me, curling them on my g-spot while sucking on my clit. I lost it. Holding onto his hair and scratching on the expensive sheets, I exploded into bursts of orgasm, my toes curling and body trembling.

"I'm so proud of you, baby. Such a good girl." James kept murmuring sweet praises, soothing the aftershocks and caressing me everywhere until I calmed down, slumping on his bed.

"That was too much," I whispered, nuzzling into his neck and kissing his skin. "You're mean."

He chuckled and cupped my cheek, blue eyes sparkling. "You still loved it."

I blushed and kissed him. "I did." Feeling him poking underneath me, I wriggled my hips and said, "You can come in me like last time."

His eyes darkened, his hands tightening on my waist. "Last time like in the Halloween?"

I swallowed and nodded remembering the scarily hot role-play sex. I had suggested the idea, and he had put the mask of Ghostface that I had given him to good use after scaring me before pinning me down to fuck me. He had given me a creampie and fucked me again just to make sure before dropping the role and taking care of me.

It was one of the best sex I've ever had, but then again, I always felt like that after sleeping with him.

He lightly patted my ass and kept me down on the sheets. "You were complaining about being sore this morning."

I whined when he left the bed. "Please—"

"No, Princess." He used his stern voice, making me pout. "I'll fuck you tomorrow."

I licked my lips, staring at his ass when he walked into his ensuite to shower. Smiling to myself, I laid back on his massive bed and sighed. It was not my fault he looked so sexy when he came back from the gym. I just had to jump on him, and he had returned the favor by teasing me for an hour straight.

Things were going so well that I almost couldn't believe it. Dad was still unsure about our relationship, but he was laughing and smiling with James and me during our Saturday dinners. School was going well, especially after the Halloween party. I was considering telling James about my feelings. He had even shown me around his penthouse, which looked more like a bachelor pad with lots of plants.

I trailed my finger over one of the leaves and donned a robe when cold breeze kissed my bare skin. I looked around his bedroom, skipping over the dresser where he had sneakily bought and kept my deodorant and all the makeup I used. It made me feel so happy that he wanted to make me feel comfortable at his place and even bought me too many clothes, placing them in his closet.

I picked up a photo frame where he looked young and goofy with baggy clothes but a poker face. His eyes were intense and somehow, he seemed unhappy as he glared at the camera. A cozy home was in the background.

Setting it down, I hummed a tune and opened the drawer to find some clothes to wear. I could steal another one of his hoodies or a tee shirt and hopefully he won't notice. Well, even if he did, he'd just playfully punish me.

I stiffened, seeing a plain file with a newspaper clipping. It looked very familiar. I pulled at it, covering my mouth, when I saw the car wreck. Images of my mother lying in bed flashed in my head, the weight of Dad's hand on my shoulder, his cries. Blinking, I looked down and read the news again and again. I knew my mom died during Christmas, losing control on one of the icy roads and crashing her car but...

"What do you want to have for dinner, Princess?" I jumped hearing his voice, and turned around to see him rubbing his damp hair with a towel, a small smile on his face. Until he looked at my face and frowned. "What happened?"

My chest was heaving, and I was finding it hard to breathe. "H-how?" I asked and shook my head, stepping back when he tried to touch me. "Why?"

"You're turning pale, Mia. What happened? Are you sick?" He tried to touch my forehead, concern lacing his face.

"Don't touch me." I moved away, squeezing the paper in my hand. "How do you know my mom? My dad? Tell me," I demanded.

His eyes flickered to my hands, his throat bobbing as he swallowed. "I didn't want you to find out about it like this, Princess."

"Don't you dare call me that." I pushed the paper on his chest and glared at him. "Tell. Me."

"Mia, I…" He closed his hand around me, his eyes roving over my face. "I was reckless. I was drunk My mom was driving and…" His lips quivered, his hand tightening around my hand, but I pulled away.

"Did you…?" I choked on the question. I didn't want to think about it. I couldn't even imagine him getting in the same accident that killed my mom.

"I got drunk and started fighting. My mom picked me up, and she was scolding me and then… I remember sobbing and apologizing to her," he said, pulling out the file and showing it to me. "I tried to get your mom out of the car, Mia. I swear. I really tried, but her belt was stuck and…"

A sob tore out of me and I fell on the floor, covering my face. I knew what happened next. He didn't have to say it. The car had blown up, and they still kept her bruised body in the bed, trying to make her breathe while my dad cried, holding my hand. My mom died in the same car accident. So did his mother.

"Mia, please, look at me," he whispered, his voice straining, kneeling across me.

"She went out to buy me a present—" I choked, fat tears rolling down my face. "I was being stubborn about not receiving any gifts, and she kissed me and Dad, promising me… promising me she'll come back with presents." My dad was smiling so affectionately at her, tucking her hair behind her ear and whispering her to drive slowly while I grinned at them. I remembered Dad baking a cake, talking to me as we patiently waited for mom. And kept waiting. For hours. Until Dad got anxious when she wouldn't answer her phone.

"I'm sorry." I glared at him through the tears, my heart breaking all over again. "I'm sorry, Princess. Please believe me—"

"Dad knows, doesn't he?"

"Clyde was the only one who didn't blame me." His hands were shaking, clenching them into fists. "That fool asked me why I had been drinking and paid for my car and tuition."

I swallowed the lump in my throat. That sounded like something Dad would do. Show kindness, offer it even when he was breaking apart. I reached out and touched James' hand, holding his cold palm in my hands, stroking his cold knuckles.

"Why were you drinking?"

He took a sharp breath. "Because my dad was hitting my mother."

41
OWN GOOD

JAMES

Saying the words out loud felt like my skin was ripping apart and my body was on fire. The sound of my mother's wail after the harsh smack kept echoing in my head. What horrified me the most was that mom was keeping it a secret for years wearing turtlenecks in summers and wearing heavy foundation when she wasn't going anywhere.

"H-he didn't stop," I managed to say through my gritted teeth. Her warm hands caressed my hand as if I deserved it. "I remember punching him. There was a lot of yelling and shouting. Mom locked herself in a room when he finally left the house to get more drunk in a bar. I followed him, getting into a serious fight until my mom picked me up."

I couldn't meet her eyes.

I chuckled grimly. "That was my Christmas, Mia. I grabbed a bottle—*fuck*, I don't even remember what I had been drinking. I was just angry. At everyone. And then Mom scolded me the entire ride. Not that piece of shit who hit her —" I swallowed when her small fingers entwined with my hand, squeezing it.

I didn't deserve her. I didn't deserve her pity, sympathy, care, love, anything at all. Even her hatred felt too precious for someone like me.

"After the accident, Clyde helped me. I got away from my father—he didn't even care that Mom had died, but Clyde was there for me. I was finally glad to live. I didn't want to study, but your father was stubborn, so he put me in college. He was the first person I called when I got my first paycheck, when I got promoted, when I bought this penthouse."

I finally tried to meet her eyes, tears trailing down her cheeks as she stared at me. "Your mom made me a promise to look after Clyde and her daughter, who had the biggest sweet-tooth, Mia."

More tears rolled down her face, and I leaned closer to wipe them away, her hand clutching her heart-shaped necklace. I pulled away, resisting the urge to hold her in my lap and apologize to her.

"I'm sorry." She shook her head and stood up. Her legs were shaking as she turned away from me, getting dressed in her jeans and sweatshirt. "I-I need to go."

I stood up, my heart aching. I understood her. I did. But fuck it, I just wanted to hold her and never let her go. I clenched my hands to stop myself and asked, "Do you want me to drop you?"

She raised her eyes at me. Her lashes were wet with tears and she was biting her bottom lip from quivering. I held myself back from taking a step towards her and protect her. But I couldn't protect her from myself. Because I was the reason she was crying with such a vulnerable look on her face.

"I-I need to get away from you, James." I stiffened, waiting for her to hurt me but she never did. "I need some space. To think and process all of this. I'm sorry."

"Goodnight, Princess." My voice was barely audible.

My entire body was rigid and tense as I watched her leave, walking out of the room without saying another word. Maybe it was for her own good. She deserved better. Someone who wasn't the reason of her mother's death. Someone her age. Someone who wasn't her fucking teacher.

Someone other than me.

It was for her own good.

* * *

Mia

It was hard trying to process that the man you loved might be the reason your mother was six feet underground.

But talking to Dad had helped. He had never been angry with James for what he had done, he was only angry with his father, and James had lost his mother, too. He didn't even blame him for the accident, joking that Mom was a clumsy driver, so it could never be entirely James' fault or his mother's.

I hated that Dad was so forgiving and kind. Because despite being his daughter, it hurt every time I looked at James in front of the classroom, talking about dimensions.

The day when I was ready to forgive and confess my feelings to James was one of the worst days ever.

There were police cars with blue-red sirens when I arrived at school. My heart dropped to my stomach and my hands went clammy as I placed my things in my locker. Only worst-case scenarios ran in my head.

James getting arrested. Cops taking him out of the school, sending him to prison for sleeping with me. His reputation turning to dust and his company going bankrupt.

"Did you hear about—*dude*, you look like you've seen a ghost."

I turned to Summer, my tongue feeling like lead. "I..." I blinked hard when I heard the shouts coming from the dean's office. "What's going on?"

Emma joined us, leaning back on her locker and going through her phone. Compared to me, she seemed like she just had a vacation in the Bahamas. "Our dean slept with a minor and accidentally uploaded the videos on Pornhub."

My eyes widened and lips fell apart when she showed me the screen of her phone. I scrolled through the article, cold horror and disgust spreading across my body. Someone had sent all the evidence directly to five of the biggest news journalists and the police, giving them enough material to sue and make the arrest.

"That's gross." I shuddered, giving it back. "Did she really do that?"

Summer nodded, frowning at the ceiling. "I feel really bad for the freshmen. They were being blackmailed."

"Wait, more than one—"

Emma squeezed my shoulder. "Let's go help the other students. We are raising awareness about sexual abuse, signs of grooming and how to spot a pedophile."

I nodded, tightening my hold on the textbook I was holding. "I'll help in any way I can."

Before we left, we all saw James, Miss Laxmi and the other teachers exit the dean's office with grim-looking faces. I pursed my lips when his blue eyes roved over me. My eyes averted to the dean, who looked like shit with her grey hair ruffled and mouth set in a scowl. She glared at all of us, keeping her chin high even when the cops dragged her with her hands cuffed behind her.

"Come on." Emma held my arm and shot a dark look at James when we passed him.

It was going to be a long fucking day.

* * *

"Mia."

I bit my lip and looked at him. "See me after class, please," he said, before giving us homework for the finals that were coming soon.

Knots of nerves jumbled in my stomach when I waited for the class to finish. Rumours of other teachers blackmailing students and abusing them had spread around, and a few of the students were making bets on which teacher would be found next. No wonder James wanted to talk to me after the class.

"I'm sorry you had to see all that in the morning," James said, clearing the board and raking a hand through his hair. He had bags underneath his eyes, and his eyes weren't clear. It looked like he hadn't slept in a while.

"Are you okay?" I asked, touching his hand.

He flinched, clenching his hand. "Sorry. I don't think we should do this anymore."

My heart stuttered. "Do what anymore?"

"*This*." He bit out. "Whatever our relationship is. It has to stop, Mia."

"I know it must be hard for you, but you are not her—"

"It was me." His eyes blazed with anger as he said, "I was the one who found out about all the shit she did."

My lips fell apart. "Y-you sent that to police and... *ohmygod*. How long have you known?"

"It's my fault, Mia." He rubbed his face. "I had a private investigator on her, and I knew she was sleeping with a student. He wasn't a minor, but then my PI dug deeper to find some dirt on her and found out about it. If I had done something sooner..." He shook his head. "I should've done something. I'm just as bad as her."

"You're not!" I took a sharp breath, holding his hand.

"You're not Eden because she is a pedophile. Think about it. If you didn't send that evidence to cops or journalists, she'd still be a dean, and trying to hurt more people... more students."

James pulled his hand away. "That doesn't change what's going on between us, Mia. We are done. Forget about me."

My eyes stung hearing his harsh words. I won't let him do it. Stepping closer, I cupped his cheek and made him look at me. "Look at me, James. Look at me and tell me you don't want me anymore. That you want to forget about me."

He still didn't.

"Look at me and tell me you don't love me." My voice broke when his ocean eyes flickered to my face.

"*Princess...*" he whispered, cupping my cheek, wiping my tears. "I can't say that."

"Then—"

The door of the classroom opened, and we weren't quick enough to pull away. Claire looked at us both, gaping at us. "I knew you were fucking him, you bitch."

42
IT'S OVER

MIA

Every vein in my body turned cold when I saw the evil expression on Claire's face. I pulled away from James, who looked more distant than anything. As if he had already expected to be the next teacher who walks out of the school in handcuffs.

I would never let that happen to him.

"I've heard the cops are still interviewing the students." She smiled, and it was nothing but cruel. "I'll be sure to let them know about you two."

She turned before I could explain. I went to follow her, but James held my wrist.

"*Don't*," he pleaded, "Let her be. I knew the consequences when I kissed you for the first time, Princess. It's okay."

"I can't." I shook my head, my throat clogging at the thought of James getting hurt because of something that was our decision. "I'm not going to let anyone hurt you."

I pulled away, running after Claire. I had to stop her and somehow convince her with a lie. Maybe I could tell her that he was hugging me and consoling me.

"I'll make you suffer." I heard Claire's voice coming from

the chemistry lab and poked my head in there to find my best friends standing across from her. "My mom will hear about this!"

"Mia!" Summer beamed. "We found this birdie trying to spread rumours about you and Mister James. So scandalous!"

I frowned in confusion and joined them. My eyes widened when I found tears rolling down Claire's face. "Why are you crying? Are you hurt?" I turned to Emma and noticed her poker face. *Oh, no.* "What did you guys do to her?"

Claire slapped my hand away when I tried to dab away her tears with a handkerchief. "I don't want your help." She glared at both of my friends and sniffled, "I'm sure someone will believe me—"

"I'd love to see you try, darling," Emma said, tilting her head and nodded at the door. "Now scurry away before I change my mind."

Surprisingly, Claire obeyed, running out of the lab.

I turned to them. "Change your mind about what?"

Summer smiled and pulled me into a hug. "Nothing you should worry about, sugar. Come on, I've heard they're serving ice cream in the canteen today."

"But—"

"*Shh.* Let's go."

I was ignored and dragged into the canteen. If Claire had cried because of my friends, then... they were both evil geniuses. I shuddered, thanking my stars that I was their friend and not a foe.

I should let James know. Pulling out my phone, I sent him a quick text,

Me: Situation is under control. Everything's okay. Can we talk?

I waited impatiently checking my phone and tapping my foot up and down. He read the message. I waited with bated breath when a typing bubble popped up.

James: It's over. I'm sorry, Princess.

I quickly pressed the call button. I didn't care if I was in the canteen and surrounded with other students. I wasn't going to—

"*Motherfucker.*"

Summer and Emma dropped their fries and looked at me with wide eyes. "Did you just curse?" Summer asked, squinting at me. "Are you sure you are Mia?"

"He broke up with me," I whispered, my vision getting blurry. "He said it's over."

Emma embraced me, shushing me and rubbing my back while Summer cursed him like a pirate while I cried between them like a bloody loser. I couldn't even confess to him. Tell him that *he* was the present my mom gave me.

I wished I could hold him again and talk to him.

* * *

A few weeks later

I SIGHED HEARING the same robotic response when I tried calling James for the umpteenth time. He wasn't even replying to my emails and only helped me during the class when I had a question. Turning off my phone, I glared at my project sitting on my desk.

It wasn't due for months, but I had made it in anger and heartbreak over James' absence. He had asked us to create anything we wanted and I knew mine would be the simplest and the most un-creative project because I had made a house. A home. I had folded the thick paper until I had seen the walls of the house and kept folding and gluing other paper until it was done. A cozy little home with a chimney, a backyard with pool and a car in the garage. I had even painted it with acrylic color so it would look homier.

I gently pushed it away so I could bang my forehead on the desk. A long sigh escaped my lips as I wondered why James had to break up with me and why I left him that night at his penthouse. Would we be still together if I had stayed?

Checking the time, I stood up and made my way downstairs.

"Hey Dad, hi Carter," I greeted the two men, smiling at the physical therapist who was visiting our house three days a week to help dad with his exercises. "How's it going?"

"He is giving me hell." Dad grunted, stretching his leg and slowly standing up. It brought a smile to my face. He could walk for a longer time, and his legs didn't hurt even if he stood for a couple of hours, even though I scolded him about it. "As usual."

"He's doing much better. His hips are still a little rigid, but I don't think he needs me anymore." Carter titled his head and grinned at my dad, "Unless you want to pay to look at my charming looks and equally charming companionship."

Dad grumbled something as Carter left, leaving me staring at our rug. I took a deep breath and said, "James told me about the accident, Dad."

I heard him take a sharp intake of breath and peered at him when he took a seat in the armchair. "Is that the reason... you two?"

"Broke up? I don't know." I pursed my lips, sitting cross-legged on the couch and tucking my feet underneath me. "I think he blames himself for what happened. Then the next day, he broke up with me over a text and has been avoiding me ever since. I don't know what to do, Dad."

"Oh, Pumpkin." I looked up at him and he was smiling sadly at me. "James never talks about his past to anyone, especially that accident. It took months just for him to open up to his therapist."

"Then why does he hate me?" I asked, wrapping my hands around myself.

"He doesn't hate you."

"He's avoiding me like I'm the black plague."

Dad took a deep breath and met my eyes. "He thinks that he murdered two people, Mia. His mom and Joyce. Do you know why?" When I shook my head, my heart thundering loudly, he continued, "Because he thinks that if he hadn't been drinking or gotten into a fight, his mom and Joyce would still be alive. His mom wouldn't have gone to pick him up, and they wouldn't have argued in the car and… I think he is scared of losing you, Mia."

My lips wobbled, but I kept my hand clenched on my arm, mulling over my dad's words. "I never blamed him. I never blamed him for the accident, but I can't tell him that, Dad."

I heard the armchair creak when he stood up and felt the light ruffle on my hair.

"Give it time, Pumpkin. I'm sure he'll come around. He can't miss our special Saturday dinners forever."

I nodded, taking in a shaky breath and biting my lip. I'd have to give him time and love him from distance.

43
HAPPY BIRTHDAY
JAMES

I stared at the night lights of the small town that had become my home for the past couple of years. It wasn't covered in snow anymore and winter's harsh wind had turned to soft, cooling breeze in the evening. I trailed my finger on the glass, reminiscing about the time I had Mia pinned against it and made her come over and over again until she slumped in my arms, smiling at me with such a raw, giddy expression that I had taken her again on the floor.

My throat tightened and I downed the whiskey, relishing in the sharp burn it offered. I deserved more than just that burn. I looked around the empty house and yanked my tie away, hating each breath I took. I paused on my way to glare at my drafting table scattered with blueprints and the design of new hospital in New York.

Images of Eden, ex-dean of Saint Helena, flashed in my head. The numb, poker face of the freshmen who averted the cop's gentle face when they prodded him with questions that no kid should ever be asked. Only if I had done something about it sooner... only if I hadn't been drunk that night or gotten in a fight...

So many only ifs and what ifs.

I couldn't be with Mia, my Princess, anymore. That was final. No matter how much I wanted her or needed her... sometimes wants or needs weren't enough. I wonder if my love for her would ever be enough. I chuckled to myself, *how could it be?* She was eighteen and had a full life ahead of herself. She deserved to be with someone of her own age who wasn't the cause of an accident that took her mother's life.

Before I could pour myself another drink for such a sad, pathetic day, my eyes flickered to the iPad where I saw a familiar lithe frame on the screen. It was a live feed from the front of the building and I saw Mia, with her dark silky hair, holding a box in her hand.

My jaw clenched as burning ache spread through me. I punched receptionist's number and snapped, "Tell her no one's home."

Without another word, I ended the call and watched the feed when Mia was stopped by the receptionist, her brows furrowing and arms hugging the box she was holding to her chest. My eyes hurt seeing the raw hatred and pain flicker on her face. I could tell she was going to cry. I couldn't see it anymore. My head hurt. My heart hurt.

But finally, she left. Stomping through the floor and never turning back.

I slumped on the stool and stared at the auburn liquid in my glass. At the start of the year, I was confident that nothing would happen between Mia and me. Now, I was begging to touch her, hold her for a fleeting moment before I leave.

I downed the whiskey and said to myself, "Happy Birthday, James."

* * *

A few months later
Mia

MY FACE WAS poker when our economics teacher kept babbling about spreadsheets. It was the last day of school. Our finals were over and we had to show our models to James. The best from each class would get the chance to have a paid internship straight after college at Fox Constructs.

I looked out of the closed glass window. Wind swept the empty branches of the trees. Leaves were scattered around on the ground and some of the kids in our uniform were laughing and playing football.

I hadn't talked to James since the day our dean got arrested. He hadn't come to any of the Saturday dinners or visited us for Christmas and New Year. When I drove to his penthouse to give him cake for his thirty-sixth birthday, his receptionist said he wasn't home. I left crying, almost throwing the cake box on the floor.

He hadn't responded to any of my messages, voicemails, or calls. When I tried to ask him questions during the class, he would answer coldly and never stayed alone with me even when I just wanted to talk to him.

Even though Emma had threatened to cut his balls, he didn't care.

He didn't want me. It was over.

I took a deep breath when I entered the class and froze, seeing Miss Laxmi instead of James.

"Where's Mister James?" I asked, holding the small model I had made.

She smiled at me. "He left the school. I've been asked to check the projects even though I don't unders—"

"What do you mean, left the school?"

She frowned at me. "He quit. He was here on a contract for two years, but he terminated it."

"Why?" I pressed, my heart pounding in my ears.

"I'm not sure what the exact reason was, but the student board said that he got an offer from one of his clients in New York, so he quit early." She shrugged, "If I were him, I'd do the same—"

I turned around and left the class. *James quit.* He wasn't my teacher anymore. He received an offer, and he was leaving for New York.

I called him, but of course, he didn't pick up. I called my dad, and he picked up on the fourth ring, "Hi, Pumpkin—"

"Where's James?" I asked, not caring that other students were staring at me when I started running. Struggling to hold the model and pulling out the car keys from my skirt. "Is he leaving for New York? Is he at his office? His house? Tell me, Dad."

"*Oh.*" He seemed sad. "I think he sent me a text last night about some flight, but I didn't think he was serious."

My blood ran cold. "What flight, Dad?"

"Wait, I'll send it to you." I heard his friends talking in the background. I almost forgot about his big hockey event. "I've sent the—"

"Thank you, Dad!" I unlocked my car, throwing my backpack and model in the passenger seat. "I'm sorry for disturbing your big game."

I took a sharp breath when I noticed his flight leaves in thirty minutes. I checked the map on my phone, and my eyes went blurry. It'd take thirty minutes to drive from the school to the airport.

These past few months had been a wreck without him. If he didn't want to be with me then it was fine. But I wouldn't let him act like a coward and run away from me to New York. *I'll make him talk to me and if he doesn't listen, I'll ask my friends for help, kidnap him, tie him up and make him talk.* I was done being ignored.

I buckled my seatbelt and revved up my car.
I could make it in twenty minutes.

44 CALL ME DADDY

MIA

Spoiler Alert: I didn't make it in time.

The flight had taken off fifteen minutes before I reached the airport. I demanded the security to let me make sure it hadn't. I started sobbing when they threatened to call my parents and school—I was still in uniform.

There was tightness in my stomach, a painful numbness in my chest. *I couldn't stop him.* I wanted to dig a hole for myself and never get out of it. I hated that I couldn't stop him. Hated myself for ever leaving him alone in that bedroom after he had confessed everything to me. James must have felt guilty for all these years and instead of helping him, consoling him, I added fuel to that guilt-fire by leaving him.

I was staring numbly at the crowd of people when someone cleared their throat.

I raised my eyes to see a beautiful woman smile at me. "Do you mind if I sit here?"

"Sure. Sit. Sleep." I shrugged, wiping my face. I didn't know when I had started crying. "Do whatever you want. Life has no meaning."

She chuckled, and it was a warm sound. "And why do you think life has no meaning?"

I pursed my lips and looked at her golden-brown eyes. She looked sincere enough, and I didn't care as I opened my mouth and spilled everything about James and the sad end to our relationship. "So yeah. He ran away. Just like that. I have enough savings to book a first-class ticket to New York, but—"

"It's okay. Calm down, love." She patted my hand and offered me a soft smile. She had dimples. "Do you really like this man?"

"I love him," I said, my cheeks flushing underneath her intense gaze. Embarrassment clogged up my throat as I whispered in a small voice, "I couldn't even tell him that."

"And do you think he has the same feelings as you?"

"I would guess so." I bit my lip from quivering. "But I couldn't even ask him if he does."

She hummed. "Have you thought about going back home?"

I frowned, but she continued, clearing her throat when adorable blush slashed her tanned skin, "When I was struggling with something really difficult, I thought my boyfriend would leave me. But he never did. He was waiting for me to open up to him and accept his love all that time."

"And... did you guys make up?" I asked with raised brows. "Did you confess?"

"We did." She grinned, golden flecks flickering in her brown eyes. "So, you should go back, love. He might be waiting for you."

"I leave you alone for one minute..." a husky voice muttered. My lips fell apart when a tall, broad shouldered, hot man walked towards us. He looked familiar in a celebrity sort of way, his hair onyx and eyes of different color. "We have to board, Kiara. Elijah and Aethra are waiting for us. You know how much—"

"Don't be grumpy, Ethan. I was just making sure this sweet girl found her happily-ever-after." The woman stood up and smiled at me, her hand glinting with the golden band. "I hope you find him and accept his love."

I nodded robotically when the hot man named Ethan finally looked at me, gave me a polite nod, and looked at his wife again. If I had a hot partner like either of them, I'd probably do the same, but his eyes practically melted when he looked at her. I could see that he adored her.

I wanted what they had. I had to go home.

"I will," I said, standing up with new determination. "Thank you, Kiara and... Ethan."

My drive back home was fueled with nerves and anticipation. I was scared, yet confident. There was a chance that it was too late and James would never wanted me back but... there I believed that he would take me back with open arms. I just had to confess and accept his love. If what Miss Laxmi said was true, then we could be together. He wasn't my teacher anymore.

It was a beautiful day. The sun had set down, painting the sky in beautiful shades of blue and pink.

I don't remember when and how I parked my car in the garage. How my legs trembled when I opened the main door and how my breathing stopped completely when I entered the house.

"James."

He looked over his shoulder, wearing a 'Call me DADDY' apron and holding a spatula in one of his hands, the watch I gifted him glinting on his wrist. "Took you long enough." He turned back, stirring the pot and acting so nonchalant as if I hadn't just had a mini-heart-attack. "Come on in, I'm cooking your favourite dish."

Turns out, the stranger at the airport was right.

"You're a jerk," I said, launching myself on him and burying my face in his chest despite his protest. I took a lungful of his pine and musky scent. I never wanted to get away from him again. I missed him. His steady heartbeats, his scent, his warmth. "I should hate you. *No*. I *do* hate you. I hate you, I hate you, I hate you."

His arms tightened around me, pulling me closer until we were pressed close. The tightness in my stomach eased and instead turned into a fluttering mess. My heart was hammering and my legs were shaking at the awareness of *him*. James. And how much I loved him. And how I couldn't stand being without him.

"I'm sorry for realizing it too late, Princess," he whispered, raking his hand through my hair and kissing my head. I felt the warmth of gentle kiss spread all over my body. "I-I was afraid I'd hurt you. That maybe you deserve someone better."

I pulled away to look at his face. His jaw was clean shaven and his sapphire eyes were sparkling when he smiled down at me, his hands cupping my face. "I'm sorry it took me so long to realize that I can be that someone better. I'll do everything and anything to be the right person for you, Princess."

"You already are, James." I kissed his hand, nuzzling into his palm. If I were a cat, I'd be purring. "I don't want you to change. I love you as who you are." I considered what I had just said and added, "Maybe you can cook some more junk food..."

He kissed me and my entire world shattered. Then he kissed me some more, and it felt that life was not so meaningless after all. His lips were soft, and I melted against him, feathering his hair and touching him everywhere. It felt like years had passed since he had kissed me, and I never wanted to feel that sadness again. I never wanted him to stop touching me and kissing me.

"I love you," he whispered, between our kisses. "I love you, I love you, I love you."

"I heard you the first time." I nipped at his lips, giggling when he hoisted me up in his arms. When I saw where he was taking me, I wriggled in his arms.

"You made it?"

He nodded, pulling away from my neck to lay me down on the blanket fort. It had a string of fairy lights and even chocolates on the side with pillows and blankets. "Clyde called me and told me what had happened."

"I thought you were really leaving," I mumbled, unbuttoning his shirt.

"I couldn't. The thought of leaving..." he shook his head, his eyes following my fingers when I tugged off my uniform. His words were hoarse when he whispered, "I'm too selfish to let you live without me, Mia."

I kissed him again, our fingers tugging at each other's clothes. I gasped when he laid me down on my back, both of us as naked as the day we were born.

His eyes zeroed on the dainty heart necklace. He smiled, brushing his fingers over it. "I'm sorry I couldn't get you anything better."

I clutched it, my lips parting. "Y-you... you were the one who gave me this present?"

James kissed the spot below my ear, licking the hammering pulse on my neck. "I gave it to your dad. I couldn't look at you after seeing you in the hospital room. It was all I could afford at that time." He kissed my lips, making me feel drunk and dizzy with his small, soft kisses. "I'll buy you a better one."

I shook my head, too stunned to speak. "N-no, I love this. I want this."

Confess to him.

Swallowing the lump in my throat, I whispered, "I love you."

My lips parted in a soundless moan when James slowly slid inside me, squeezing our entwined hands and groaning my name as we joined as one. He took his time, slowly dragging himself out and slamming inside me with deeper thrusts, making both of our bodies jolt on the pile of blankets.

"James... Daddy, I love you," I moaned, scratching down his back when he pressed deeper, rubbing my sensitive bundle of nerves and making me explode.

"Cum for me, Princess," he groaned in my ear, his pace increasing as I felt his release near. "Cum for your Daddy."

I did, holding on to him and crying out his name as my orgasm took over me, shaking me to my core. I moaned in his neck when his warm seed filled me up, caressing his back when he shuddered, dropping over me.

"I love you," James whispered, kissing my forehead and looking at me like I was everything and more than he wanted.

And the world was perfect again.

THE END

READ EXPLICIT BONUS SCENE HERE
Or type this link into your browser:
https://mailchi.mp/bac1b0de57a8/bonusscene

Thank you so much for reading Tempting Teacher! If you enjoyed reading this book, I would be grateful if you could leave a review on the platform(s) of your choice.

Reviews help other readers like you find this book and are hugely appreciated by authors!

Love always,

Mahi

EPILOGUE

MIA

"Ah—"

"That's it, my sweet dirty princess." James grunted, his length filling me up in one fluid motion. "That's it. *That's it.*"

"Daddy…" I sighed, melting into his arms when they tightened around me. My half-lidded eyes met his ocean-eyes, so clear and sharp.

He slammed into me.

My lips parted in a soundless moan at the pleasure of his cock stretching me and brushing against the g-spot. My fingers scrunched his shirt when he increased his pace, his warm breath fanning on my cheek when he pressed against me, lifting me effortlessly in such a small space.

"Such a good girl," he crooned in my ears, squeezing my waist when I tried my best to stifle my moans.

"I'm gonna come…"

"Cum on my cock, my sweet princess slut." Pleasure tightened in knots inside me, his length throbbing and pulsing. "Cum. For. Me."

His hand covered my mouth, and I had to bite down on his hand when I exploded with pleasure. His thrusts became rampant when my walls spasmed around him with orgasm, prolonging it as much as he could before releasing inside me. He squeezed me so tight that I was sure I'd bear the marks of his fingers on my waist for a few days.

My eyes flickered open when he erased all the distance between us, pressing his forehead against mine. I smiled, raking a hand through his hair and pulling him closer. My smile only widened when he whispered the sweetest words ever that I had been dreaming of since I was sixteen.

"I love you, Mia." His lips brushed against mine when he whispered again, "I love you."

"I love you too." I was grinning, kissing him and floating on cloud nine and basking in the post coital bliss in his arms.

There was lots of shuffling and bumping into each other when he retreated to straighten up his clothes. But his eyes hardened, retrieving the lace panties which dangled from my right heel.

"I'm keeping this." He said, sliding it in his pocket and straightening my dress, having a feel of my ass. I swatted it away, hot blood warming my face.

"I'm sore. A-and we should hurry—"

I opened the stall door and flushed harder at the reflection of my mussed hair and smudged lipstick. I didn't know James would follow me into the washroom when I had excused myself from Emma's birthday dinner. He had acted innocent, that he was just checking up on me, making sure I didn't need any tampon or pad... and as soon as I had said no, I wasn't on my period, he had pounced on me like a starved animal. Locking us both in a bathroom stall and ravaging me like a beast.

"Princess, if your friends don't suspect I was fucking you, then I haven't done my job properly." James leaned against the tiled wall, looking handsome as ever with striking eyes,

EPILOGUE

dark hair and the sexy look on his face that said 'I'm ready for round two when you are.'

"You are crude." I made sure I had cleaned up as much as I could before sneaking out of the washroom.

"Sorry." I murmured, sliding on the cool leather seat and glancing around the table to see Emma and Caleb sharing a small heart-shaped chocolate cake while Summer wriggled her brows at me.

"Quit it."

"I didn't even say anything!" She batted her lashes, trying to act innocent.

"We all saw a possessive, demanding, and totally whipped sugar daddy boyfriend run after you when you went to the washroom." Emma smiled at me, looking over my shoulder where I was sure James was seated for his 'meeting.' Summer even waved at him, which made me want to crawl underneath the table and hide forever.

"I still can't believe he is... you know." Caleb shrugged, taking a sip of champagne. He had planned the dinner in the three Michelin star restaurant. They both had made up recently, and he had woken up Emma with cheesy music blasting through her backyard and asked her out. Even though I didn't entirely disapprove of him, I didn't understand their relationship.

"If you had asked me a year ago that James would be my boyfriend, I'd have laughed at you... but here we are." I smiled, sneaking a glance over my shoulder to see him watching me. Butterflies swarmed in my stomach.

"He even gave me a pretty birthday gift." Emma said, reminding me how he had gifted her a set of cooking books because he loved to diss at her. I didn't understand their animosity, either.

"Do you have any plans fo—"

Emma's phone rang, and I frowned when her expression

EPILOGUE

became cold and heartless. It was the same expression she gave to everyone who didn't know her. Her tone changed when she picked up the phone.

"Who do you think called her?" Summer asked when she walked away from the table, speaking quietly.

"Who else?" Caleb stared at her back and glanced at us. "Her mom."

When Emma didn't come back to finish the dessert with her boyfriend after a few minutes, we all grew worried. My stomach was in knots when I saw her pale face. She was clutching the phone in her hand. The phone call had ended, yet her stony expression remained.

"Em? Is everything okay?"

Her eyes drifted from the marble floors to us.

"My mother... she's dead."

PREVIEW OF DON'T DATE YOUR BEST FRIEND

KIARA

"If you don't want to kiss me then . . . let's swim."

"Yeah, sure."

"Naked."

"*What?*"

"I always wanted to try skinny dipping." I pursed my lips and said, "And I really want to get out of these clothes."

When I thought about it, I wasn't feeling self-conscious about my body when it came to him. Yes, he had seen in me in bikinis and accidentally walking in when I was busy writing something on my Post-it in my underwear and bra. But I was never self-conscious about what he would think of me or my body. I did have stretch marks, but I wasn't uncomfortable about them. What I was most worried about was *myself*. If he got naked and my hormones spiked up, I didn't know if I would control myself and not jump on him.

Gosh, I sounded so bad in my head. Not to mention, my best friend would be the first guy I would ever see naked. *Way to go, Kiara.*

His voice was strained when he said, "What if someone catches *you* . . . me, both?"

I moved my damp hair over my shoulder. "We will be in the pool, Ethan. And no one can see us from the living room." I smirked when I said, "Unless you want to watch me while I swim, you can stay here."

The thought of Ethan watching me with his intense green-blue eyes while I was swimming naked in the pool sent a delicious shiver down my core.

His eyes darkened and he looked away, probably thinking the same when I noticed red blush creeping up his neck and making his ears and cheeks flush. *Cute.*

I prodded, "Come on, Ethan. Don't be a chicken..."

"*Fine.*"

He stood up, his tall frame towering me. I forgot how to breathe when his dark eyes seared me, slowly trailing down my body as if he had all the time in the world. His voice was rough when he said, "Remove that sweater first."

I raised my eyebrow at the sudden change in his demeanour.

Ethan said, "You have an extra piece of clothing than me."

I grinned. "Who said I was wearing any underwear?"

I loved the way his pupils widened in shock, surprise and then they were clouded by scorching desire. Biting my lips, I whispered, "I was messing with you."

Holding the hem of the sweater, I tugged it up and removed it. I straightened my damp hair and shivered. But it wasn't because of the cold air.

His eyes averted down my breasts, which were barely covered by the ivory lace bralette. As it was wet, he could easily notice my hardened nubs, which were begging for his attention.

We were crossing a dangerous line right now. And I knew neither one of us wanted to step back.

"Your turn," I managed to whisper.

EXCLUSIVE CONTENT

Want more exclusive content? You can sign up for Mahi's Patreon to read steamy one shots every Saturday!

As a supporter, you get access to early drafts, exclusive VIP content, deleted scenes, deleted chapters, cat pictures and YOUR NAME in the Acknowledgements of my books.

www.patreon.com/mahimistry

ALSO BY MAHI MISTRY

Have you read them all?

Alluring Rulers of Azmia Series

Dirty Wild Sultan

Filthy Hot Prince

Tempting Rebel Princess

Charming Handsome Sheikh

Alluring Rulers of Azmia Complete Series Books 1-4

The Unfolding Duet

Don't Date Your Best Friend: Best Friends to Lovers

Don't Date Your Ex Best Friend: Second Chance Best Friends to Lovers

The Unfolding Duet Books 1-2

Dominating Desires Series

Twisted Therapist: Brother's Best Friend Age Gap Romance

Tempting Teacher: Student Teacher/Dad's Best Friend Age Gap Romance

Scan to easily access all of my books:

ACKNOWLEDGMENTS

Thank you so much for reading Tempting Teacher.

Thank you to all my beta readers, editor, proofreader, arc readers, bloggers and book lovers, bookstragramers, I couldn't have done this without you. Especially Jeanie. You helped me a ton with this novel and I'm so honoured to have you as my editor. Edie, you're a gem! I adore you and our conversations.

Thank you to everyone who accepted the ARC edition of this book and helped me share this book with the world.

If you enjoyed reading this book, please don't forget to leave a review. I would really appreciate it. It helps find more readers like you and they are very important for authors!

Special thanks to my Patrons: Christina Derrick, Jennifer Styler, Melanie Antogiovanni, Stelladxnna and Michele Mills.

ABOUT THE AUTHOR

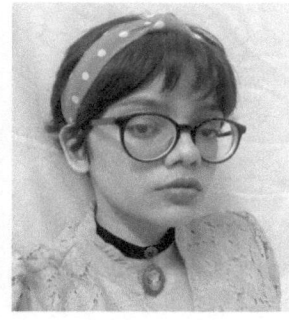

Mahi Mistry has been writing since she was in middle school. Soon, she fell in love with writing passionate, steamy romances. Her stories have elements of humor, suspense and character development. Mahi's main purpose in her life is to make one person happy every day, even if that is a stranger reading her book and rooting for the main couple or her cats by giving them extra treats.

She enjoys simple things in life, like spending time with her family and friends, cuddling with her cats, reading and writing drool-worthy characters while sipping on hot chocolate from the wineglass to validate herself that she is actually an adult. She is an avid reader of fantasy, romance and thriller books and thinks writing about yourself in third person is atrocious. She firmly believes that cats rule the world.

www.mahimistry.com

www.ingramcontent.com/pod-product-compliance
Lightning Source LLC
LaVergne TN
LVHW041906070526
838199LV00051BA/2514